tuned in

EPISODE #2

# star struck

## by Julia DeVillers

Printed in the United States of America

First edition, 3rd Printing

ISBN 0-9678906-7-5

Visit www.limitedtoo.com

# introduction

OK, so this is the deal. Right this very second, I am sitting on an airplane. And guess where this plane is heading ...

HOLLYWOOD! Oh yeah, Hollywood, California. Like, where TV shows are filmed. Where TV shows with famous TV stars starring in them are filmed. Like where TV shows with famous TV stars starring in them are filmed that I get to go watch happen.

Yes, me! Maddy Elizabeth Sparks! Flying off to watch a television show being filmed and meet some TV stars!

Is this a normal thing that always happens to me? Because I'm so glamorous? Oh puh-lease. I have never done anything exciting in my entire life ... up until ten days ago. That's right, it was just ten days ago when I was all bummed out because I didn't make cheerleading. And all my friends did. And I wondered if I'd lose all my friends and be alone for the REST OF MY LIFE!

And then Mom took me to the mall and I got stuck in the bathroom with three girls. Kacey. Isabel. And Claire. We got "discovered" by these people from Limited Too headquarters.

And they said we could help them with all this stuff so they'd know what girls like. And my life totally and completely changed in that one afternoon. We got to go to headquarters and be models in their catazine.

Like that wasn't major enough?!?!

It just keeps getting cooler!
More exciting!!
More awesome!!!

Because I'm off to Hollywood! Yes, THE Hollywood, California. Home of TV stars, movie stars, singer stars ... stars, stars, stars, stars and more stars! And ... for a few days, ... home to ME, ME, yes, ME! And also ... Kacey! And Isabel! And Claire!

We're going to the land of the stars!!!!!!!!!!!!!!!!!!!!!

AHHHHHHHHHHHHHHHHH!

It's crazy. I mean, just two days ago, I was hanging out with my friends, watching them at cheerleading practice. I had no idea I'd be off to HOLLYWOOD.

How is this possible? How could it be true?

Well, let me tell you what happened.

# chapter 1

**This Journal Belongs to:**

Maddy Elizabeth Sparks

PRIVATE!

KEEP OUT!!

Zack, THIS MEANS YOU!!!!

See, I knew I could get over it. I knew I could get over feeling totally bummed out that I didn't make cheerleading. I'm proving it to myself right this second. That's right, I'm sitting here on the school lawn watching my friends practice for football cheerleading season.

You might say I am the cheerleader for the cheerleaders.

Handsprings and splits! Walkovers and round-offs!

Toe touches and herkies! They're flipping! They're flying! They're cart wheeling! They're ... crashing! YIKES!!

Oops. Major collision. Now Brittany's yelling at everyone to watch where they're going. She's team captain.

Now they're starting a pyramid! Four cheerleaders on the bottom ... three climbing on the next row ... two more climbing on the next row ....

And Brittany's climbing on top.

"Go Brittany, go!!!! Woo hoo!!! Go Pom-pom girls! You rock!!"

Hey. That was a pretty good yell I just did.

_Almost cheerleader quality, I'm thinking. This isn't so bad. Hanging out in the sun ... sitting on my blanket ... writing in my journal. Think I'll just lie back and watch the show now. More later._

So, all right then. It's not so bad that I'm not out there with the cheerleaders. Not so bad to be sitting on the sidelines.

Maybe even better to be sitting on the sidelines right now. Because um, guys ....

The pyramid is looking kinda shaky. Kinda wobbly. Not very steady ....

OH!

The pyramid is collapsing! Everybody's falling! Oof! There's a big pile of cheerleaders on the ground. A huge tangle of arms, legs, pom-poms everywhere! Ouch.

And now ... everybody's fighting. "Who screwed it up?! Who knocked over whom? Whose fault was it?"

Whew. I'm thinking this cheerleading team needs to

work on its teamwork.

"Come on you guys! Get up! We need to do that again! And get it right this time!" Brittany was screaming from somewhere inside the pile of cheerleaders.

"I'm thirsty," one of the cheerleaders called out. Then it got kinda crazy.

"I'm tired!"

"Can't we just sit down for a minute and take a break?!"

"Owwww! I bruised my knee!"

"Bruise on your own time!" Brittany yelled back. "Come on! Get up! No time for drinks! No time for breaks! We need to do another pyramid!"

I took a sip from my water bottle. Ahhh. I wasn't thirsty. I lay back on my blanket. I wasn't even a little bit tired. I was not bruised. I closed my eyes, enjoying the sunshine.

I thought about how when Danielle called and invited me to come watch cheerleading practice, I wasn't sure. Maybe I'd be too jealous. Maybe I'd be like, "What about meeeeee? Let meeee cheer, too!"

Or maybe everyone would be like, "Um, why is Maddy here since she didn't make the squad? She should be embarrassed to even show her face around here."

But nope! When I got here, everyone was glad to see me! So see? Everything's cool. I'm still one of the girls. Ha. Me worried about being left out? Not even. No problemo.

VROOOOOM!!!!

My eyes popped open. What was that noise? Sounded like an engine starting. Hey wait a sec. All the cheerleaders are taking off. They're all running to the parking lot and climbing on a minibus and ....

"HEY!! HEY!!!! Wait for meeee!!!"

✳ ✳✳✳✳✳ ✳

"Sorry, Maddy," Brittany said to me, as we ate our pizza in a booth at the pizza place. "We totally forgot you were there."

Oh yeah? Gee, what was my first clue? Maybe when the whole cheerleading squad ran off and jumped on the minibus taking them to get pizza. Or when the minibus pulled off and didn't wait for the girl running after it. The girl waving her journal and yelling, "Hey! Hey! What about me?"

The only girl not in a green and white cheerleading uniform.

**Red-face Rating:** ★☆★ out of ★★☆★★ stars. *They're wearing bright green uniforms. I'm wearing a bright red face. Sigh.*

At least the driver finally saw me and stopped. And oh yeah, THAT was fun. Climbing up the bus steps and walking down the aisle. Acting like it was no big thing.

But I KNOW everyone was staring at me like, "That's soooo funny! We forgot all about Maddy!"

Augh. I'm forgettable.

Well, at least now I was sitting at the pizza place with everyone else. Sharing a booth with my friends, Brittany, Haley, and Danielle. Scarfing down a slice of pepperoni. That whole "forgetting about me" thing is SO over. Right?

Augh. Augh. AUGH!!!!!!!! ☹

"But Maddy, I'm so glad you're here," Brittany said to me. "Because I've been doing some serious thinking. I need the complete and total scoop from you. Tell me EVERYTHING. How you pulled it off."

"Um, pulled what off?" I asked.

"You know, how you got to be a model," Brittany said. She twisted her long white-blonde hair around her finger as she talked.

"Yeah, how you got to be a model," Haley echoed.

"I already told you guys," I said. "I got locked in a bathroom with three other girls. And then later this woman from Limited Too headquarters just came up to us at the store. And asked us to help out. I mean, I wasn't picked because of my natural supermodel looks or anything."

"Obviously," Brittany said and laughed. "Just KIDDING!"

Gee thanks.

"Well?" Haley said.

Everyone was looking at me.

"What?" I said. They were still looking at me.

WHAT?!!!

"Duh, Maddy," Brittany said, putting down her drink and looking me right in the face. "You know we've been best friends since like forever. You, me, Haley, Danielle, and Taylor before she moved away. Don't you think you're being unfair, here?"

Um, huh???

"Um, huh?" I said it out loud this time.

"Well, what has my dream been all my life? What have I always, always wanted to do?" Brittany asked.

"Be a cheerleader?" I guessed.

"Well, yeah, that too. And I'm so happy to be one now, of course" Brittany said. "But I also want to be a model. You know I've always wanted to be a model."

"So, here's the deal! You need to get Brittany into modeling!" Haley said to me. Brittany gave her a smile.

Did they rehearse this or what?

"Well, you guys," I said, slowly. "You know I really want to help. But I mean I wasn't really a real model or anything. Just for that one day. I'm not sure how real modeling stuff works."

I didn't want to make Brittany mad. But it wasn't like I

could just say, "OK! I'll make a few calls." And then tada! Brittany would be a model.

Oooookay. They were all still looking at me.

"So!" I said cheerfully. How about a change of subject! "Only two more weeks and then ... back to school!"

"Yeah, yeah, but wait! You have to get Brittany into modeling," Haley said.

Uh oh. Change of subject not working.

"Maddy," Brittany said. "Think about it. It's totally unfair that you get to be a model and I don't. When it is my life's dream. And you've never, ever said you wanted to be a model. But then you got to be one. So how unfair is that?"

"It's totally unfair!" said the Echo. I mean Haley.

Then Danielle spoke up.

"Actually, it's not really unfair," she said. "I mean, I'm happy for Maddy. Something cool happened to her this time. I mean, we all got picked for cheerleading. But Maddy didn't. It all kind of works out in the end."

I smiled at Danielle. I really needed that.

"Um, Danielle?" Brittany said. "I think you might be misunderstanding the situation here. Because it's not like we had anything to say about who made cheerleading. We didn't have inside information on how to become a cheerleader. Like Maddy has about modeling."

Uh oh. I started chewing on my shoulder-length medium brown hair. Chew. Chew. Mom told me if I kept chewing my hair when I was nervous, she'd chop it all off. Chew. Chew. Chomp.

Brittany kept talking.

"So see, Danielle? It's an entirely different deal. Isn't it? Isn't it, DANIELLE?"

Gulp.

This was bad. Worse even than it might sound.

Because Brittany was using THE VOICE.

I thought of it as THE VOICE. Because it wasn't like a regular voice. It was the one that said, "I'm used to getting my own way. And don't stand in my way." This was not good. When Brittany used THE VOICE, it just was so not good.

The first time I'd heard Brittany use THE VOICE was at recess. In second grade.

We always swung on the same four swings: Brittany, Chelsea B., Danielle, and me. Until the day Chelsea and Brittany got into this little fight about who was going to have the better birthday party.

"You're always such a showoff," Chelsea B. said to Brittany. "You're just jealous because I'm having a moon jump."

I watched as Brittany's eyes narrowed. She dragged her feet until her swing stopped.

"Um, Chelsea?" Brittany said. "I don't think you understand. You're having a moon jump. That's so kindergarten. I'm having a DJ. So see who's going to have a better birthday party? See? See?"

And she said that in THE VOICE.

The next day on the playground, Chelsea came over to the swings. I was on one of the swings. Danielle was on another. Brittany was on the third ... and Brittany had put her feet up on the fourth.

"Oh, sorry, Chelsea" Brittany told her. "This swing's taken today."

"By your feet?" Chelsea asked, all confused.

"That's right! Sorry!" Brittany said cheerfully. "No swing available today!"

Chelsea looked at Brittany's feet on the extra swing. Chelsea looked really sad and went over to the monkey bars. And never really came back. The next day, Brittany invited the new girl Haley to take Chelsea's place on the swing. And in our group.

So that was way back in second grade. I snuck a look at Chelsea B. sitting with some other cheerleaders eating her pizza. It was a long time ago, but I still felt kinda bad about that day. I wondered if I should have said something. Stuck up for her. Yeah, but I mean I was only a little kid. I didn't have much of a clue back then.

I've got more of a clue now. I was kinda surprised though. I just hadn't heard THE VOICE for soooo long. And not used on one of our own group!

So even though we're not little kids anymore, THE VOICE was still, well, sorta scary. I looked at Danielle. She was nervously playing with the beads on her braid. And staring down at the table.

Of course! I know, I know that's the right answer. That's what I should have done. But it just seemed easier to let it go. Nobody gets mad, Danielle's off the hook, Brittany's happy .... Let's just get the whole thing over with. Move on!

How did this all start?!! OK. Brittany wanted me to help her get into modeling. I didn't know what I could possibly do to help her but ....

"Hey Brittany," I said. "I'll think about what I can do to help you model, OK?"

Brittany smiled at me. And then smiled at Danielle.

Whew! Crisis OVER!

"SO!" I continued. "Two weeks till school starts! Summer's almost over!"

# chapter 2

The day had started OK. My horoscope was good:

> **Libra:**
> *Be prepared for an unexpected surprise! Prepare for a trip in your future! Your friends will be right there with you!*

Well, my horoscope had sounded like it was supposed to be good. A surprise! A trip! With friends!

But blugh. The way my day actually went, not good. My horoscope should have read:

> **Libra:**
> *Be prepared for an unexpected surprise* **when your friends all take off on the cheerleader bus without YOU.**
>
> *Prepare for a trip in your future* **to get pizza, although you almost missed even THAT.**
>
> *Your friends will be right there with you!* **Yeah, friends like Brittany. Greaaaaaaaat.**

When I got home I was in a B. A. D. baaaaaaaaaaaaad mood. I needed to cheer myself up! Yeah, right! I needed to do something relaxing to forget about my yukko day! Right? So what should I do? Something totally fun?

Oh noooooo. Mom said it's chore time.

So I'm in my bedroom. Finishing the dreaded task. Ugh. Ugh. Ugh.

Cleaning my guinea pig's cage.

OK, it's not that I don't love Sugar. She's a cutie pie little fluff of brown and black fur. She makes that sweet little snuffly noise when she's happy.

BUT I HATE CLEANING HER CAGE! IT'S SOO GROSS!! P. U.!!

Now, if I had a dog, there would be no cage to clean. OK, there might be some stuff to clean but still. I would do it! I wouldn't even complain about it! I would do anything for my dog!!!!

If I had one.

Mom? In for a dog. Zack? In. Dad? Out. "Too messy," he says. "Too furry. Too much of a hassle."

But I'm working on getting Dad to change his mind. Once again, this morning, I'd brought him the morning paper with a big smile. The newspaper folded to a page with an article I'd circled with my blue gel pen. It was about this retirement home for senior citizens. And how these volunteers from the animal shelter bring dogs to visit the people there. And how it cheers them up and makes them all happy.

Dad glanced at the page. And said, "Thank you for the paper, Maddy. Are you trying to hint at something here?"

Yes! Yes! That we should get a dog! That we HAVE TO get a DOG!!

"Are you suggesting I'm ready for a retirement home for senior citizens?" Dad continued. "Because I think I've got a little time before that's necessary."

"No! Dad, this part!" I pointed to the paper. "How dogs make people happy! See? There's, like, research on it and everything!"

"Thank you for sharing, Maddy," Dad said. "But what would really make me happy right now is for you not to bother me about getting a dog today."

OK. No luck today. But, I think he's softening. I really do.

So for now, I have a guinea pig. I put Sugar back in her clean cage. I ran downstairs and threw the bag of Stink in the garbage.

WHEW! That stink seriously STANK.

So did my day. I'd been left out and left behind. I'd heard THE VOICE. I'd promised to help Brittany become a model and yeah like I knew what to do about that. I even had to do Stink Patrol.

"Sugar," I said out loud. "Could something even a little bit good happen to me today? Anything, anything at all?"

OK. Now I'm the crazy girl who asks her guinea pig for help. I need to regroup!!!!!!! I need a break!

I need to get away! I need to have some fun in my life!

"Maddy," my mom stuck her head in the door.

"What now?" I snapped. "I need to scrub the bathrooms?"

"No, you need to change your attitude. And then talk on the phone," Mom answered, handing me the receiver.

Rah. Whoopee. Not! It's probably Brittany wondering if her supermodel contract was ready.

"Hello?" I said into the phone, still in grouch mode.

"Hi, Maddy. It's Lauren from Limited Too," I heard.

"Oh! Hi, Lauren!" I said. I lost the grouch mode fast! Because Lauren worked at Limited Too headquarters. It was here in my town. Lauren was the one who had first invited us to help her out at the company. Lauren was sooo nice.

"I have your next Too Crew assignment," Lauren said. "Your parents have already given their permission. I think you're going to enjoy it."

And this is what Lauren told me:

> ☆ Limited Too was holding a bunch of contests.
> ☆ And the first one was "Win a Day In 'The Zoe Zone'"!
> ☆ The Grand Prize Winner gets ...
>> ○ A makeover, a cool new outfit from Limited Too!
>> ○ AND a trip to Hollywood, California to go on the set of the TV show, "The Zoe Zone"!
>> ○ PLUS the winner gets to meet the stars of the show. Like Zoe Montana!!!!! And Austin Hamilton!
>> ○ AND the winner gets to actually be in an episode of the TV show as a character!!

How cool is that contest?!!!! I'll tell you how cool ...

WAY COOL! I'd already heard all about the contest. Some girl out there in the universe was going to be reallllly lucky.

But I didn't know this next part.

The Too Crew was going to help out with the contest, Kacey, Isabel, Claire, and me. And that meant ... we were going to Hollywood.

"OK, WHAT?" I said.

"Yes, it's true. You're going to Hollywood, Maddy Sparks," Lauren said. "So pack your bags. Because we're leaving tomorrow."

OK, wait a minute, here.

I WAS GOING TO HOLLYWOOD? WITH KACEY, ISABEL, AND CLAIRE?!!! TOMORROW??!

I can't even believe this. Is she serious?

"Are you serious?" I asked her. "Tomorrow?! As in *tomorrow*, tomorrow?"

"Yes, it's pretty last minute, isn't it?" Lauren laughed. "But we had some late changes in the contest with the winner. The winner isn't able to bring a friend with her. So this is what I'm thinking:

- ☆ The Too Crew could come keep her company
- ☆ You girls could be her Welcome Committee
- ★ Then she would have other girls around, too.

If you're interested, that is?"

Interested? INTERESTED?!! Hm, let me think about it. Am I interested in going to Hollywood, California?

"AHHHHHHHHHH!"

"I'll take that as a yes," Lauren laughed. "I already discussed the game plan with your parents. All four of you girls get to go. So ask your parents for the details and I'll see you at the airport tomorrow."

Ohmigosh, Ohmigosh. I'm going to Hollywood? Tomorrow? Ohmigosh. This is so unbelievable. What do I do??!! Where's my suitcase? What do I pack?

Help! MOOOOOOOOOOOOM!

# chapter 3

OK. I'm packed. I have a seriously stuffed suitcase full of clothes. And my backpack with my:

- ★ Sunglasses! 'Cuz it's sunny in Hollywood! Plus I need to look all glamorous, right?
- ★ Lip gloss #1 -- clear and kind of sticky feeling!
- ★ Lip gloss #2 -- pinkish strawberry!
- ★ My blue fuzzy journal and blue gel pen!
- ★ Pepper! My cute fuzzy black Build-a-Bear! That my BFF Taylor got for me!!!
- ★ This great new book I'm in the middle of!

And now ... I am ready ... TO GO TO HOLLYWOOD!
HOLLYWOOD HOLLYWOOD HOLLYWOOD HOLLYWOOD

Sorry. I just can't stop saying that.

HOLLYWOOD HOLLYWOOD HOLLYWOOD HOLLYWOOD

OK, I'm done. Seriously.

# HOLLYWOOD!!!!!!!!

OK, OK. I'll really stop that now. But how psyched am I?

WAY psyched!

Me + Trip to Hollywood = WOO HOOOOOOO!

Times a bazillion!!!

I mean and once we get there? Being part of the whole "Zoe Zone" thing? I mean, "The Zoe Zone" is such an awesome show. Like, how Zoe Montana plays Zoe, the awesome athlete. And she has the best teammates! So nice! And so like, "Yay, Zoe!" No matter if they win or lose they're like, "Yay, Zoe!" They're always there for her!!!

And then ... there's Arthur.

Ahhhh. Zoe's best bud. He's totally the opposite of her. Uncoordinated. Hates sports. Arthur is supposed to be a geek. But I think he's waaaaaaay cute.

Arthur is played by this actor, Austin Hamilton.

He's #4 on my crush list. Numbers 2, 3, and 4 were all famous people. But #1 is ... shhhh! Ryan Moore.

Yes! Ryan Moore!

He's not a TV star or a movie star or a singer. He's a

regular guy in my school. Well, not exactly regular. Dark brown hair. Dark blue eyes. And way cute.

He was in my math extra-help class last year. And I saw him once this summer, too. At the mall that day I met Kacey, Isabel, and Claire. And he said to me, "See you at school, Maddy."

Yes! Ryan Moore talked to me! Me!!!

And I will see him at school! And when I do, I'll be ready.

I'll be like, "Oh, hello." La, la, la, no big deal. Talking to Ryan Moore like he was just anybody. I'll be all like this:

"Oh hi, Ryan. How was the rest of your summer?" Then he'll say, "Good. And how was yours?" And I'll say, all cool-like: "Great, thanks. So what's your schedule? Maybe we have a class together this year."

Yup. I'd been practicing. I had it memorized and good to go. So the next time I saw him, I didn't just go like this: "GAH."

Not that that would ever happen or anything. Ahem.

Yes! I was practicing! Soon I'd be able to talk to any guy! Without saying "GAH"! Even a guy on my Ultimate

Crush List!!!!!!!

OK. I'm hoping anyway. For now, I'm stuck talking to one guy. And one guy only.

My little brother, Zack. Who just walked into my room.

"What do you want, Zack?" I eyed him suspiciously.

Previous Times Zack Has Come into My Room:

- ★ He read my journal (Remember to check that the key is still in its NEW hiding place).
- ★ He put gum on my pillow.
- ★ He took all my Barbie's and cut their hair off (OK, that was back when I was six. But I'm still MAD).

So. I am watching him. Closely. Verrrrry closely.

"So Precious Maddy gets to go to stupid California with some stupid girls," he said. He reached into Sugar's cage and pulled her out. "Like you're ever gonna be any kinda help for a contest or whatever. Yeah riiiiiight. They must be desperate or dumb! Pathetic."

Sugar started kicking her legs and making that guinea pig noise, "SQUEEEEE!"

"Zack, hold Sugar's legs! You're freaking her out," I told him. "Look, I'm busy packing, OK? I have things to do. So get out."

Zack put Sugar on my bed, next to my suitcase. And he flopped down on my bed.

"That's NOT getting out," I pointed out.

"So you get to go to California and hang with all the TV stars," Zack complained. "Me, I get to stay here and have Mrs. Hubert BABYsit me when Dad's at work. This is so lame. Whoopee for me."

Oh. That is a bummer. Mrs. Hubert was like a gajillion years old. Which would be OK if she wasn't like, "That's enough video games! You hold the yarn for me while I knit you some mittens! And no junk food! I made you some nice spinach and raisin cookies." Nasty!

That DID stink. Poor kid. Oh, now I felt bad for Zack.

For like ONE MINUTE. Because all of a sudden I saw something moving in my suitcase.

Yes, MOVING.

A worm! There was a long slimy worm in my suitcase!

"ZACK! Get that worm out of my suitcase!" I yelled. "Oh, shoot," he said, jumping off the bed.

"Busted."

He ran out of my room. I threw a pillow at him.

"MOM!" he yelled from the hall. "Maddy's throwing things at me!"

"Guys!" my mom yelled. "I'm trying to get everything ready. It would help if you two would get along for just two seconds!"

AUGH!!!!!!!

I got a tissue and picked up the worm, careful not to touch it. EWWWWW. I hope it didn't get any worm juice on my clothes.

"GROSS!!!"

I could hear Zack laughing hysterically. Oh, ha, ha, ha. Laugh away, Zack.

Have fun with Mrs. Hubert.

Buh-bye.

# chapter 4

"We need Gate B4. OK, there's Gate B1, B2, and B3 ..." my mom said to me. Mom and I were at the airport, on our way to our gate, on our way to our airplane to ...

# HOLLYWOOD!!!

I looked around to see if I could find Kacey, or Isabel, or Claire. I hadn't seen them since the day we went to Limited Too headquarters. We'd e-mailed like, "Hi! Wonder what the Too Crew will be doing next!" That kinda stuff. But now ... we'd all be back together! And I was excited! But ... I kinda was feeling that nervous feeling. 'Cuz maybe everything would be all weird. Maybe it would be all awkward. I just hope they're happy to see me.

"There it is!" Mom said all cheerfully. "Gate B4!"

There it was! And there THEY were!

ISABEL!!!!!!! And KACEY!!!! And CLAIRE!!!!!

Here I go! Walking over their way! And then they saw me. And were like, "MADDY! MADDY'S HEEEEEEEERE!" Yeah. I RAN over to them.

Kacey was jumping up and down. Isabel was smiling. Claire gave me a hug. And we all looked at each other.

And I yelled, "We're going to ..."

And we all looked at each other. And then YELLED ...

# HOLLYWOOD!!!

"Ahh, the Too Crew is reunited again," Lauren called over to us. "Hi Maddy!"

"Lauren drove Kacey and me here," Isabel said. "Our parents couldn't come because of work," Isabel explained.

Isabel was her usual total Hip Chick. She was wearing a navy blue tank top, skirt, and some platform shoes. She had little clippy things in her long, dark, curly hair.

"I can't believe we're going to 'The Zoe Zone'"! Kacey said in her bouncy voice. "I never miss that show."

Kacey had her straight black hair up in spiky pigtails like the day at the catazine shoot. She was wearing a T-shirt that said "Hoops" on it, matching pedals, and white sneakers.

"Hey, you guys are wearing your charm bracelets, too!" I said. We all held up our wrists together. My glass slipper charm! Kacey's soccer ball charm! Isabel's sunglasses charm! Claire's cell phone charm!

"Where are you guys sitting?" I asked them. "I'm in seat 14A. Is anyone next to me?"

"Me! You're next to me! I'm 14B!" Kacey said.

"I'm in 14E," Isabel said.

"I'm not sure what seat I'm in yet," Claire said. "I'll have to check my ticket."

"The trip's going to take like four hours," Kacey said.

I can't imagine Kacey sitting in one place for four hours! Or even four minutes!

*"All first class passengers to Los Angeles are now invited to board,"* the loudspeaker said.

I noticed Bruno getting on the plane.

"Is Bruno getting on now?" I asked Claire.

"Yes, my dad moved him up to first class," Claire said.

"He gets too squished in coach."

Yeah, Bruno is pretty tall. But hey, I'm happy to be in any seat at all! On a plane with Kacey! And Isabel! And Claire! Sweet!

"We're in luck! It's not too crowded," Lauren walked over and handed Claire a ticket. "We got you a seat next to Isabel's. It's 14D."

"Didn't you have a seat?" I asked her.

"Well, kind of," Claire said.

"Her father had her moved up to first class," Lauren told us. "But she asked me to switch her ticket."

"What are you crazy?" I asked her. "You could go first class? Wow! You could get all that celeb service."

Claire shrugged. "It's no big deal. I'd rather sit with you guys."

I'm serious. That Claire is way nice!!!!! Oh, and did I mention seriously supermodel gorgeous? Her straight, long blonde hair was pulled up in a knot kind of thingie. She was wearing light blue pants, and a white tank, and a cardigan. And light blue strappy shoes.

"I love your hair thing!" I told Claire.

"This? Oh? Do you want it?" She reached up to get it.

Oh yeah! I forgot! If you compliment Claire, she'll try to give you her stuff! Can you say TOO generous?

"Claire, you're NOT giving me anything this whole trip!" I warned her.

"Oh. Sorry," Claire said. "Oh no! But wait! I HAVE to give you something. I brought one for everybody!" She pulled out a bag of candy bracelets. She gave one to each of us.

"Hey, candy charm bracelets!" Isabel said. "Like how we have our Too Crew bracelets."

"Look, it has a heart charm dangling from it!" I said.

"The heart made me think of us all being friends," Claire said, shyly.

Claire is waaaay nice! And waaaaay thoughtful.

The announcements started. *"All passengers in rows 10 and higher are now invited to board Flight 1971 to ..."*

we all yelled again!

IT WAS FINALLY TIME TO GET ON THE PLANE!

!!!!!!Maddy Goes Hollywood!!!!!! (That's me!!!)

"I wonder what movie they're going to show. I wonder if they serve peanuts or pretzels. I like pretzels better but peanuts are OK," Kacey chattered, from the seat next to me. She was talking a gajillion miles a minute.

I had a window seat. Claire and Isabel were right across the aisle. My mom and Lauren were in the row in front of me. They were just talking away.

"OK, I have a plan," Kacey said, talking loud enough for Isabel and Claire to hear. "We'll break the flight up into thirds. First, Maddy and I will sit together. After an hour and 15 minutes, we'll switch. I'll sit with Isabel and Maddy will sit with Claire. For the last hour and 25 minutes, I'll sit with Claire and Maddy will sit with Isabel. I'll set my watch."

OK, HUH?!!! What did that girl just say?!!

I looked at Isabel and Claire and we started cracking up!

"What?!" Kacey said.

"Oh. Nothing. Just that you're very organized," Isabel said. "No wonder you're such a good team captain."

Kacey was captain of her soccer team and basketball team. Oh, and her track team, too.

"Thanks!" Kacey said, smiling and doing something to her sports watch. "OK, my timer is on. Ready, go. OK, Maddy, our turn to talk."

Kacey pulled a pack of SweeTarts out of her backpack.

"Want one? They're the chewy kind. I have the other kind, too, if you want those, too. Purple's my favorite in the chewy ones but I like red a lot too!"

I took a couple SweeTarts. Kacey passed them around.

"I've never been to California!" Kacey said. "Have you? Isabel did once. Claire goes all the time. She travels all over with her father! Like to India! Spain! Hong Kong!"

Wow. I'd only been to Florida. And just twice. Those were the only times I'd been in a plane. Claire's gone all over the world? Wow and wow.

**Places Maddy Would Like to Travel**

☆ Australia (to see some cute koalas!!!!)
☆ New York City (shopping!!!!)
☆ Paris ('cuz I'm taking French in school this year!
Parlez-vous something something?)
☆ Hollywood (to see the Stars! And hey! Here I go!)

The plane started to move down the runway. There was a loud roar and the plane lifted off the ground. Up, up, up ...

We're going up! I looked out the window and watched as we circled over Columbus. Everything looked so teenie. Hey! I think that's the water tower right by my house!!!

I gave a little wave at the window. Hi, Dad! Hi, Zack! Hiiiiiii, Mrs. Hubert! Heh heh.

OK, that's not very nice. Heh, heh.

"Want a magazine?" Kacey asked me. She held out some.

I flipped through them. Basketball! Softball! Tennis! Sports, sports, and more sports!

"You are seriously sporty," I said.

I am seriously NOT sporty. I had tried. I had won an

award. Once. OK, it was for "Best Attendance." Meaning, "She showed up. But that's about it."

"I just looove sports! Just like Zoe!" Kacey said.

Yeah! Kacey IS a lot like Zoe. All sporty and "go team!" while I'm more like Arthur. Basically a klutz. The girl who didn't make cheerleading, who walks into doors with her face, who jams bathroom doors.

"I can't believe we're helping with 'The Zoe Zone' contest!" Kacey said. "I wonder if we can know who the winner is. Let's ask Lauren." She poked her fingers through the gap between the seats in front of us.

"Pssst!" she said. "Lauren! We have a question for you!"

"What's up, girls?" Lauren asked, turning around.

"We were wondering about the winner of 'The Zoe Zone' contest," Kacey said. "Like what her name is and stuff."

"Let me tell you all about her," Lauren said. The "Fasten Seat Belt" light was off. She came and sat in the seat next to Kacey. "The winner's name is Jennifer. She's a little younger than you and from Arizona. You'll be meeting her at the restaurant this evening."

There were a bunch of winners. Some of them won cool stuff like CDs, clothes, and videos! But only the grand prize winner was going to ...

"How did you pick the winners?" I asked.

This is what Lauren told us:

- ★ You had to tell why you wanted to win a day in "The Zoe Zone." In 25 words or less.
- ★ Limited Too collected all the entries and read them.
- ★ They narrowed down the finalists.
- ★ And then they picked the one, the best, the most perfect **GRAND PRIZE WINNER!**

"That sounds hard! I mean, there must have been zillions of entries," Kacey said.

"It was very hard!" Lauren agreed. "There were so many great entries. But we narrowed it down by scoring for different categories like originality, creativity, and sincerity."

How cool would that be! I mean, to have someone all official call you and your parents and say,

## "CONGRATULATIONS! YOU WON!!!"

Lauren showed me the winning entries.

**Finalist #1**
I'm not good at sports like Zoe is. But I still love "The Zoe Zone." Zoe inspires me to try my best!

**Finalist #2**
I would want to enter "The Zoe Zone" because I absolutely looooove Zoe. Plus I could show her some of my own moves.

**Finalist #3**
It would mean a lot to win. My family is real busy. But we always make sure we watch "The Zoe Zone" together!

And here's the grand prize winner!

**GRAND PRIZE WINNER - Jennifer**
I'm starting a new school. And on a new basketball team. Zoe's a TRUE friend and teammate. I want to learn to be one, too!

Yeah, Jennifer! The Grand Prize Winner! I can't wait to meet her! And help out with the contest!!!!!!!!!!!!!!

But hmmm. How AM I supposed to be helping out?

"Lauren, how do you want us to help?" I asked her.

"Well, usually girls get to bring a friend with them," Lauren said. "But Jennifer just moved to Arizona a few weeks ago with her aunt. She didn't have any friends to bring. So we thought it would be nice for you all to be there for her. To support her."

OK! Got it! All right! I could do that! See you soon, Grand Prize Winner!

I closed my eyes. Just for a second. Yawn!

Zzz ... zzz.

# chapter 5

"So maybe I do like peanuts better than pretzels," I heard a voice saying. "Usually I want them to hand out bags of pretzels on the plane but these honey roasted kind are actually pretty good and ...."

"Mmmf," I said. Whoever was talking was interrupting me. I was busy. I was playing softball with Zoe Montana. I was up to bat. And suddenly, Brittany was there saying it was her turn to bat. And why didn't I ever let her bat. And then my bat starting wiggling and turned into a huge slimy worm! And then my brother Zack was there and he was laughing and ....

"Although if they gave out little bags of chips that would be even better! So maybe I should suggest that to the airlines for snacks. Do they have comment cards?"

I opened my eyes. OK, I'm awake. That's Kacey, talking about snacks ... OK, I'm not really playing softball with a giant worm. That was a WEIRD dream. I blinked and tried to figure out where I was. OK, I'm on a plane ....

Oh! I'm on a plane to California! It seems like THAT should be the dream! BUT IT'S REAL!!!!

"Look, it's alive," Isabel said, pointing at me.

"Hey, Maddy's awake!" Kacey said. "Maddy, you slept the whole way! You slept through the movie! You slept through lunch! We're getting ready to land already!"

"Yeah, Mad, you screwed up Kacey's plan to take equal turns talking to each other during the trip," Isabel said.

"Ohmigosh! I'm sorry I screwed up the plan!" I said. "I was so excited last night I could hardly sleep! I guess I just crashed and ...."

"MADDY!" Isabel said. "I was kidding! Don't worry, Claire, Kacey and I had lots to talk about without you. We just talked about you behind your back the whole time."

Oh no.

"You DID?" I said. My heart started racing. What did they say?

"Yup," Kacey said. "We talked behind your back. Like we talked about how we have you to thank for making this all happen for us."

???

"You know, if it weren't for you, none of us would be here," Isabel continued. "First jamming the bathroom door with your nose. Then making a scene at the store so Lauren would notice us."

Oh!!!!!

They weren't talking bad about me! They were saying NICE things behind my back. Cool. My heart stopped racing.

"But really, Maddy," Kacey said. "It's true! We owe it all to you. Thanks, Maddy!"

!!!!! Awwwwww. That was all so NICE!!! Awwww!!!!

"Gakkk," said Isabel, pretending to throw up. "This has gotten way too gushy for me."

Yeah, it was way gushy. Way mushy. But I liked it.

Just then the pilot's voice came over the intercom: *"Welcome to Los Angeles, California, the home of the stars!"*

We're heeeeereeeeeeeeee!

Kacey turned around to Isabel, and Claire, and me. And very quietly said, "We are going to ..."

And we all finished it off together: **"HOLLYWOOD!!!!"**

❋ ❋ ❋ ❋ ❋ ❋ ❋

Okay, then we all got our stuff and left and did all this stuff just getting out of the plane and getting our baggage and blah blah blah boring. But it didn't stay boring for long because ...

We saw a man wearing a black uniform and cap, holding a sign that said "TOO CREW." TOO CREW! Hey, that's US!!!

"Girls, meet your limo driver," Lauren said with a smile.

Maddy needs to go somewhere. How's she gonna get there?

> a) A school bus.
> b) Rollerblades, wearing knee pads because of that last time I fell and had to get stitches, ouch.
> c) Minivan, with Zack in the next seat pinching and poking at me.
> d) An airplane and a limousine.

The answer is most definitely "d."

OK, maybe just for today. But an airplane AND a limousine! AHHHH!!!!! First the plane trip! And now I'm going to ride in a limo!!! Very niiiiiiiiiiiiiiiiiiiiiiice.

"This way, please," the limo guy said. "We have two limo's to take you to your hotel."

Hel-lo. A limo. I. Am. Way. GLAMOROUS! Would you like my autograph?

To my biggest fan, xoxox!
    Signed, Maddy Elizabeth Sparks
        (p.s. Who rides in a limo)

I put my sunglasses on. I leaned back on the limo. I struck a pose.

"Maddy, you've gone Hollywood!" Lauren laughed. "Let's make the white limo the Too Crew Mobile. We'll meet you girls at the hotel."

Yes, the Too Crew sitting in their very own limo. SWEET!

We were off to the hotel! The driver said we could buzz him if we needed anything.

The limo drove down the highway. Kacey played with the buttons on the windows. Zpppt! Up! Zpppt! Down!

"Look! Palm trees!" I said, pointing out the window. We

don't have those in Ohio! Shops! Restaurants! Gas stations! OK, we had all those in Ohio ... but these were California ones! Woo hoo!

But wait a sec ... we didn't have THAT in Ohio.

"Hey guys," I said. "Check out that woman with the red hair! That looks just like Skyler Hope."

"Skyler Hope, the singer?" Isabel asked. "Lemme see." We all stuck our faces to the window.

"It IS Skyler Hope! It is Skyler Hope!!!" Kacey said. "It IS! See that's her dog! I read in a magazine she has a little white dog and that woman is walking a little white dog and she looks exactly like Skyler Hope so ... it IS!"

AHHHHHH! We just saw Skyler Hope walking down the street! Walking her dog like this normal regular person!! And if she looked up, she would see four faces! Squashed up against a limo window staring at her! And yelling, "AHHHHH!!!!!!"

"OK, how cool is that!!!!?" Kacey said. "Like, we're just driving along and then we see Skyler Hope. How weird is that? It's sooooo ... "

**"HOLLYWOOD!!!!"** we all screamed.

I leaned back in the leather seat. I just saw a celebrity! I'd never seen a celebrity before in real life!

Except for the guy who does the weather for Channel 5. He went to college with my dad. And came over to our house for dinner once. But only once.

Because Zack was like, "So how come you said it would be sunny today? I didn't bring a coat. And it rained on me. And last week you said there would be a storm? So I skipped baseball! And I missed the game!"

The weather guy didn't even stay for dessert. The only person even CLOSE to a celebrity I'd ever seen in my whole entire life!!! And Zack scared HIM away!

BUT NOW ... SKYLER HOPE! I just saw Skyler Hope!!

I looked out the window for more famous people walking their dogs.

Zpppt! Zpppt! Kacey was playing with the buttons again. Window up! Window down! Zpppppt! Sunroof ... open!

Hey! COOL!

"Have you guys ever seen in the movies where people are riding in a limo and they open the sunroof? And stick their heads out the top and their hair is blowing in the wind and they're waving at people like crazy?" I looked at Kacey, Isabel, and Claire.

I was going to do it!

I stuck my head through the sunroof. Kacey, Isabel, and Claire tried to squeeze in with me. We were kind of half in, half out. But mostly out!

"WOO HOOOO! Hellooooo, Hollywood!" I screamed into the wind. "We are soooo ... "

**"HOLLYWOOD!!!!"** Kacey, Isabel, and Claire finished the yell with me.

WOOO HOOOO!

My hair was blowing in the wind! I was waving my arms around like crazy! WOO HOO!!!!!!! Oh yeah! Check me out! Maddy Elizabeth Sparks! So glam! So FABULOUS!

In a limo driving down the streets of Hollywood!!!!!!! In a limo pulling over on the streets of Hollywood. And ... uh ... STOPPING on the curb of a street in Hollywood.

"GIRLS!" The driver got out of the car and came around to the side. We were still sticking out of the sunroof. "I'm afraid this is a safety violation."

Oopsie.

"Uh, sorry," I tried to explain. "I just thought we could be like in the movies? Like when people stick their heads out the top? And their hair is blowing in the wind? And they're waving like crazy people ...."

"I'm afraid I must ask you to please remove yourselves from the sunroof and seat yourselves back inside the vehicle," the driver said.

Ooooookay. We all slid back into our seats.

"Sooooorry!" I whispered. "I mean, nobody ever gets busted in the movies for that!"

"Troublemaker," Isabel whispered back. And OK, we cracked up. I can't control myself.

"Girls," the limo driver's voice crackled over the intercom.

"Uh oh, what'd you do now, Maddy?" Isabel teased.

"Perhaps you wish to listen to some tunes on the radio?" the limo driver asked.

We all looked at each other. Sure!!!

"Hey!" Kacey squealed. "It's a Skyler Hope song! We just saw her walking her dog and now she's singing on the radio! That's freaky!"

"It's magical!" Claire said.

"It's soooooo ... **HOLLYWOOD!**" we all yelled.

"And let the car dancing begin!" I announced. We started moving! Dancing! Waving our arms! Bouncing in our seats! ♩ ♪ ♩

"Party limo!!! Wooooooo!" Kacey screamed.

Woo hoo!!!!! Woo hoo!!! Go Too Crew! Go Too Crew!

Yup, that's me. Maddy Elizabeth Sparks. Dancing in a limousine with the music cranked up. In Hollywood, California.

With the Too Crew!

# chapter 6

HEL-LOO *fancy* hotel!

When the limo pulled up to the hotel, my mom, Lauren, and Bruno were at the entrance waiting for us. They'd checked us in so we could go straight to our room! Up the glass elevator. To the tenth floor! To ...

"Suite 1010!" Lauren said, as we walked down the hall.

I got to the door first. Lauren handed me the key card. I stuck the key card in the slot in the door.

Brzzzt!

The door buzzed from my card. "Come on in!" I announced. I pushed on the door and ...

BAM!!

Walked right into the closed door. Face first.

Face? Meet door. Door? Meet face.

"Uh, Maddy?" Isabel said. "You have to wait till the little light on the door lock turns green before you can go in."

I looked down. The little light was red.

**Red-face Rating:** ★★ out of ★★★★★ stars.
*Red face. Red nose from slamming into the door. Red light means it's still locked, you dork!*

I turned around. Kacey, Isabel, and Claire were trying not to laugh. Lauren was biting her lip. Even my own mother was holding back a laugh.

OH. I am a dork.

Recover, Maddy! Recover!

"Um, yes! I did that on purpose," I said. "Just trying to bring back fond memories of the first time you met me. You know, when I smashed my face into the bathroom door!"

That cracked everyone up. Including me! Okay! Moving right along!

**Take 2:** Maddy Opens the Door

I pushed the key card into the slot in the door. Brrzzzt! The little light turned green. Yes, green! I looked again. Definitely green!

"Come on in!" I said again. And this time, we could! The door opened. We all walked into the hotel suite.

I looked around the suite. It was a cool setup. The living room had green and peach furniture. There was a TV, phone, computer, and little refrigerator with a fruit basket on it. And in each bathroom ... another phone, a mini tv and a humungo hot tub!!!! Ooh! Bubble jets!

Our suite is SWEEEEEET!

"I guess we should put all our stuff in our rooms," Isabel said. "And start unpacking."

Everyone started gathering their bags. And then we stood there. Because we didn't know who was in which room.

"Two to a room!" Isabel said. "It's time to pick."

Erg.

OK, you know what some of the worst words in the entire English language are? It's time to pick.

As in: "Class, it's time to pick partners for your science project." Or in gym: "It's time to pick teams." Or in this hotel: "It's time to pick rooms."

Because then you get into the whole "who wants to be with who" issue. Who wants to NOT be with YOU? And then you're sitting there going, "I hope Brittany picks me and not Haley for her partner so I don't get left out!" Or, "Please don't let them pick me last for the team!" Or at least, "I hope I'm partners with so and so!"

You know what I'm talking about! And then after you're all done picking, you have to deal with everyone going, "Oh SHE'S on our team?" Or, "I wanted to be HER partner, not yours." And blah, blah, blah, And even if they don't say it, you're worrying that they're thinking it.

Ugh. Way stressful. So, OK. We're doing "time to pick rooms." Please don't let it be "So who gets STUCK with Maddy!??!"

"I'll grab a pen and some paper and write down the numbers "1" and "2." We'll pick out of a hat," Isabel said. "The peach room is room #1. That greenish is room #2. Everyone okay with that?"

YES! Random picking! Sounds fair to me!

Isabel crumpled up the papers and held out her hands. We picked. I was a "1." Claire was a "2." Isabel was a "2." And Kacey was a "1." Done.

"Maddy and I are in peachy room #1! Go peachy room!" Kacey did a little cheer thing into our peachy room.

I started to unpack my bags. I pulled out some shirts, some tanks, some shorts. Of course, my blue and white Reeboks. Then I pulled out my outfit for dinner tonight. A cute, little flippy dress. New sandals. And ... I reached into my little jewelry bag and pulled out my fave choker.

My choker. Was moving. Yes. Moving. Hel-LO????!!

"AUHHHHHHHHHHHHHHHH!" I threw my choker on the floor! Because my choker was actually a WORM!

ZACK!!!!!!!!!!!!!!!

"What?!!!" Kacey came running over.

"My brother took out my favorite choker! And stuck in a WORM!" I screamed.

Oh ICK. For the second time in two days, I had to get a tissue. Pick up a worm. And, um, get rid of it. Major hand washing! Ewwwww! WORM SLIME!!!

"Kacey, I hope you have a little baby SISTER!" I yelled. "Unless you like WORMS!"

# chapter 7

Okay! I was wearing my flippy dress! My sandals! And no choker! Grrr ... but OK! Let's get over that. (For NOW, Zack. Just for now.)

It's dinnertime!!!

The restaurant was on the same street as the hotel, so we walked over. I was busy looking. Because you never know! Some person just walking down the street could be a TV star! A movie star! A rock star!

Because it's Hollywood!!!!!

"What are we supposed to do when we get there?" I asked Lauren. I hadn't really gotten any instructions. Was I supposed to do something? Say something?

"Mainly, Maddy, just be yourself," Lauren said. "Your usual warm and friendly self. We'll welcome Jennifer and then just talk with her over dinner. And tomorrow, I'll be with you to explain what to do every step of the way. So just relax ... and have fun!"

OK! I can do that! Sure!

We walked into the restaurant. A couple of girls walked past me.

"HEY!" I grabbed Claire's arm. "The girl with the brown hair! In the black shirt! Isn't that ...?"

Yes! It was!! It was Justice! The grand prize winner of the "America's Favorite Teen Super Star" reality show! Who sang and danced her way into the hearts of millions of audience voters!

"Look, you guys!" I whispered to Kacey and Isabel, pointing. Trying to play it cool! But how cool could I be?!

NOT VERY! I mean, I voted for that girl like a batrillion times! Till my finger was numb on speed dial!!! And now she's so close that if I tripped I would fall on her!

Oh. Maybe I shouldn't say it like that. Knowing me and all.

Maddy's Celebrity Spotting Checklist:

✓ Skyler Hope
✓ Justice, "America's Favorite Teen Super Star"
✓ The weather guy from Channel 5

WHO WOULD BE NEXT?!?!!

OKAY! Celebrity spotting over. Time to get ready for Jennifer. Our own **Grand Prize Winner!!!**

Lauren told us to head downstairs, where we'd have our own private VIP room. She'd wait upstairs for Jennifer. And she said the Too Crew should go to the room where the red carpet started. The red carpet?

COOL!!!! There was a long red carpet leading down the stairs!

"I get it! It's like an awards show!" Kacey squealed. "Jennifer's going to walk in on a red carpet!"

Oooh! And so were we! Kacey started walking down the stairs. But I grabbed a spoon off the hostess stand and ran in front of her. I blocked her from going down, holding the spoon out like a microphone.

"I'm Maddy Sparks," I announced, doing my best reporter impression. "Reporting live from the First Annual Hollywood Too Crew Awards! First up on the red carpet we have Kacey Choe! Kacey Choe, famous athlete! Kacey, how does it feel to be winning an award for um ... best sporty thing?"

"Exciting! Cool! Great!" Kacey giggled into my spoon.

I waved her on.

"Moving on, we have Isabel Vega!" I said into my spoon. "The world-famous fashion designer! Isabel, your gown is just stunning. Is it your own original design?"

Isabel looked down at her white shirt and denim skirt and laughed. She went down the stairs.

"And look!" I continued on to Claire. "It's Claire Fullerton, famous movie star! The crowd is going wild to see her!"

I looked at Kacey and Isabel. They were cracking up.

"Crowd!" I fake whispered. "Go wild!"

Kacey and Isabel cheered and clapped for Claire.

"CLAIRE! CLAAAAAAAAAIRE!!!"

Claire turned bright red.

"Claire, do you have anything to say to your billions of fans? Who are watching you worldwide right now?" I said, shoving the spoon in her face.

Claire looked at the spoon and totally lost it. She was cracking up! She couldn't say anything!

"Yes, ladies and gentlemen, Claire Fullerton! Star of the SILENT movies!" I announced.

And then, Claire laughed. But not a normal laugh. Like this big SNORT sound!

Ohmigosh. Claire! She snorted! She's so ... Princessy! OK, that made me laugh. SO hard. Claire was laughing, too.

"Oh! My stomach!" I was gasping for breath. Claire was laughing so hard she had to lie down on the red carpet.

"Girls!" Lauren called down the stairs. "Uh, is that Claire lying on the steps? Well, it's a good time to get up! Jennifer's limo is here!"

OH! OK!

Pull yourself, together, Maddy! It's time for ... **THE GRAND PRIZE WINNER**! We all ran down the stairs! OK, still cracking up a little. But under control. OK! And then we ran into our private room!

Wow!!!! There was like party stuff everywhere! Silver balloons! Gold balloons!

And huge signs ...

> ### Welcome, Jennifer!
> ### Winner of THE LIMITED TOO
> ### WIN A DAY IN "THE ZOE ZONE" CONTEST!!!!

> ### WELCOME TO "THE ZOE ZONE"! YOU ARE ABOUT
> ### TO GET ... TUNED IN!

Lauren and my mom came down the stairs.

"Jennifer's here!" Lauren called out.

She's here! She's here!

"Here's the plan!" Lauren said. "When she walks in, everyone yell 'Congratulations, Jennifer!' I'll take some pictures and then you guys introduce yourselves. OK, here she comes!"

A woman and a girl started coming down the stairs on the red carpet. The girl had short dark curly hair and big brown eyes that were wide open, like she was way surprised. She was smiling this big, shy smile.

It was Jennifer! The Grand Prize Winner!!!!!

"CONGRATULATIONS, JENNIFER!!!!" We were all clapping

and yelling!!!

Lauren went up to the girl and handed her a huge bouquet of roses. Then she started taking pictures. Flash! Flash! Flash!

Red carpet! Roses! Pictures!

"It's like she's a real star!" Kacey squealed.

Lauren waved us over. We jumped around Jennifer.

"I'm Kacey!" "I'm Isabel!" "I'm Claire!" "I'm Maddy!!!!!!"

"Can you believe you're here? Isn't this AMAZING!?" I asked her.

Jennifer nodded, like yeah!!!!

"We're so happy you're here! You're going to have the best time!" Kacey said.

"I'm Jennifer's Aunt Dee," the woman introduced herself. "It's nice to meet all of you."

"We're so happy to have you," Lauren said. "Let's sit."

I sat down between Claire and my mom. Kacey and

Isabel sat across from me. There was one seat that had balloons all stuck to it. That, of course, was for Jennifer. "Well this is certainly the most exciting thing that's ever happened in Jennifer's life," Aunt Dee told us. "I didn't know people really won these kind of things!"

Yeah! Jennifer really did!

"Winning this contest couldn't have come at a better time for Jennifer," her aunt continued. "She and I just moved to a whole new state. I know she's sad about leaving her friends at her old school. And nervous about starting a new school."

Wow! That would be hard!

"We liked your entry," Isabel told Jennifer. "About being a good friend and teammate."

"Thanks," Jennifer said, looking kinda embarrassed. But smiling, too.

"We're hoping that Jennifer makes some good friends in her new school," Aunt Dee said. "She enjoys playing basketball. So maybe she can make some new friends on her team at her new school."

I looked at Jennifer. She nodded but looked sorta sad.

Maybe she was thinking about leaving her friends.

"Well, we're your teammates for 'The Zoe Zone' Contest!" said Isabel. "And we're totally psyched!"

Jennifer didn't say anything but she was starting to smile again. Lauren called Jennifer over to the other end of the table to tell her what was going to happen.

"Jennifer's sure quiet! But she seems nice," Kacey said. "I totally hope she finds good friends in her new school."

"And for now," Isabel added. "We're going to be here for her!"

"I have an idea," Claire said to the three of us. "I thought of a present for Jennifer. I wanted to ask you guys what you thought. If you like it, we could ask Lauren.

"I was thinking, we're supposed to make Jennifer feel welcome and comfortable, right? So I was thinking that maybe we could make her part of the Too Crew. And we could get her a charm bracelet, too."

I thought about it for a second.

Get Jennifer a charm bracelet, too?!!! OK, I mean, the Too

Crew is the four of us, right? Isabel, Kacey, Claire, and me. The bracelet was just for US, wasn't it? It's special!

"I like it," Isabel said. "It would make Jennifer feel really included. Like she's a part of everything."

"And, it would be something she could keep forever!" Kacey agreed.

OK. Yeah. I'm being pretty selfish here.

"And we could have a special charm to give her, like we had," Isabel said. "How about a star charm? 'Cuz we're in Hollywood with all the stars!"

Allllllllll right. It WOULD be pretty cool to have other girls be a part of all this. Like Jennifer! And they could have their own charm bracelets. And yeah! We could keep adding new girls to the Too Crew! It would be like having friends all over! We could all have this major bond with other girls!! Forever and ever!!!!

"Cool!" Isabel said. "Claire, that was seriously nice!"

Claire blushed and smiled. Isabel was right! Claire was right! Kacey was right!

"Let's take a vote," I said. "Everyone in favor of including other girls in the Too Crew – starting with Jennifer – raise your hand!" I held up my arm with my charm bracelet on it. Kacey and Isabel, and Claire held theirs up, too. Unanimous!

# chapter 8

Oink! I pigged out at dinner! I had:

- ★ Movie Star Mozzarella Sticks
- ★ Celebrity Chicken Nachos
- ★ Hollywood Hamburger with Famous Fries!
- ★ Make Your Own SuperStar Sundae!

Now we were back in our suite. Putting on our PJs! Even though I wasn't tired yet!

Knock, Knock!

Kacey opened the door to our room.

"It's me!" Lauren said. And Isabel! And Claire! "You guys have one more thing to do tonight. You get to give Jennifer her prize basket. Plus, it would be nice to have her join you. I think she might be nervous about tomorrow."

"I'll call her now!" I dialed the operator and got Jennifer's room.

"Hi, Jennifer! It's me, Maddy! We want you to come to our room! For a surprise!"

"Um, I'm in my pajamas," she said.

"Good! 'Cuz so are we!! Come on down!!!"

We all went out to the suite. There, in the middle of the table, was the biggest, the hugest, most HUMONGOUS basket I've ever seen! It was wrapped in plastic stuff! It was tied with silver ribbons! And bows! And it had Jennifer's name on it!!!

"WOW!" Kacey said. "That thing is GINORMOUS!"

I couldn't wait for Jennifer to see this thing!!!

There was a knock on the suite door. Isabel peeked through the peephole. And let Jennifer in. And led her to the gift basket.

Hee. Jennifer's face was like ...

Huh? And then ... OHMIGOSH!!!!!!! ☺

"For me?" Jennifer said.

"Open it! Open it!" We all yelled.

Jennifer smiled. Sat down. And ... RIIIIIPPPPPP! Opened that gift basket. And then she pulled things out of it, one by one, and held them up ...

- ☆ A new Zoe Zone DVD (that hadn't even hit the stores yet)!
- ☆ Lip gloss!
- ☆ A picture frame!
- ☆ Nail polish!
- ☆ A choker!
- ☆ Chips! Candies! Gum!
- ☆ A backpack (to carry all this fun stuff!)

"That is so cool!" Isabel told her. "Some serious stuff!"

"But," Jennifer said softly. "I feel bad. You guys didn't get anything."

We didn't get anything? We didn't get ANYTHING????? OH YES WE DID!!!

We got a trip to Hollywood! With a limo ride! A night at a hotel! A dinner! With a day at a TV studio to come!

Um. I think we're doing just fine!!

While we were all saying that, Jennifer opened her gift basket snacks. She pulled the caps off the cans and poured out some snacks. She got glasses from the bathroom and poured chips in them. She spread out the candy. She put out the fruit basket that was sitting on the fridge. She turned on the stereo.

"Jennifer!" Claire said. "You set up a party!"

"For all of us," Jennifer said, shyly.

"Hey!" I said. "We're supposed to be the hostesses here! We're slacking!"

"I have new clippy things," Isabel said. "I could do your hair, Jennifer!" Isabel is good at hair. She did mine once. Seriously cute!

"There's a hot tub! You could soak your feet for a pedicure!" Kacey said. And headed into the bathroom.

"Maybe you guys can use my makeup stuff," Jennifer said.

"Hey! We'll give you a makeover!" I said. "Not that you need one or anything! Just for fun! I can do your nails!"

I'm thinking pink! Or purple! Sparkle! Shine!

"I can do the makeup," Claire said. She really didn't wear much. But she always looked so ... perfect!

Isabel on hair. Claire on face. Kacey on feet (Eww! Feet! I mean Kacey on pedicure!). And me on nails.

It's the Great Too Crew Spa Party!

"Hot tub's filling up for your feet!" Kacey said.

"Great! Let's all get started," I told Jennifer.

Polish! Clip! Puff!

"Hold still," I said to Jennifer. She was kinda wiggling.

"I have an itch," Jennifer said.

"Don't move yet," I said. "You'll smudge."

"Ooh! My nose is tickling! I need to scratch!" Jennifer said. She tried to scratch her nose without messing up her nails. She wiggled around and scratched. Hee. She looked pretty funny.

"All that scratching! You look like a monkey! With pink nails," Isabel teased.

"Oh noo!" I groaned. "Not a monkey! That makes me have flashbacks!"

They all looked at me. Ooops! Why did I just spill THAT!

"What does THAT mean?" Kacey asked.

"Yeah!" Isabel said. "What's the deal with you and monkeys?"

"Um! No story!" I said. "I didn't mean that! Take it back!"

"Oooooh, now I reallllly want to know!" Isabel said.

"Did you wear brown clothes and someone said you looked a monkey?" Claire guessed.

"Maybe it was her crush," Jennifer suggested.

Everyone CRACKED up. Including me.

"NO!!!!" I said. "OK, stop! I'll tell you!"

OK, but it's way embarrassing.

"In first grade, we did this class play. It was about a prince and a princess. And their pet monkey. And OK! YES! I played the monkey.

And Brittany played the Princess. Surprise, Surprise.

So they were having this ball at the castle. Then, the

monkey jumps on the table and wrecks the whole ball.

So, we're doing the play. And then it's time for the monkey to go on stage. Except the monkey DIDN'T go on. Because I was the monkey! And I was too nervous!"

"You get nervous like that, too?" Jennifer asked.

"Who ME? Um, YEAH! I get nervous about everything! That I'm going to screw it up! That I'm going to totally HUMILIATE myself ... and I usually do!

So Brittany kind of dragged me onstage. I was like totally frozen. But then, my BFF Taylor was in the audience. And she stood up. And waved to me. In front of everyone. And did like a monkey thing. She was scratching! She was jumping! And the audience was like, 'WHAT?'

But I started giggling. And I unfroze. I did the whole monkey thing. I jumped around. I scratched. I said in my best monkey voice: 'Eeh Eeh Eeh!' and ...'Ah Ah Ah!'

I got a standing ovation, too. Well, from my parents anyway.

The End."

I looked over at Jennifer. She was smiling.

"That's such a cute story," Claire said. "Taylor sounds really nice."

"Yeah. That's so sweet ... " Isabel said. " ... Monkey Girl."

"What did you just call me?" I asked her. "Did you just call me Monkey Girl?"

"Who me? Would I do such a thing?" Isabel teased.

"Hey! Show us how you did it! Do your monkey impression for us!" Kacey said.

No way! No how! No! Never NEVER NEVER!

"Come on! We want to see it!" They all started chanting, "Monkey GIRL! Monkey GIRL!"

And then Jennifer walked over to the fruit basket. And tossed me a banana.

Oh noooooo! Even Jennifer has turned on me!

We were all cracking up. Yeah. Me too.

"You know, our job is to do anything we can to help out our Grand Prize Winner," Claire said, smiling. "And she wants Monkey Girl."

Help! Don't make me act like a monkey! Someone rescue me! Anyone! Anything!

And then ... I heard the noise. Burble! Burble! Slop! Burble! Burble! Slop!

What was THAT?!

"The hot tub!!!" Kacey yelled. "I forgot to turn off the hot tub!!"

WATER! OVERFLOWING! FLOOD!!!! Eeeek!

Isabel ran to turn off the water! Kacey grabbed some towels!

"I need more towels!" Kacey yelled. "It's overflowing!"

We all looked at each other. And we remembered something! And we just stood there. Laughing SO hard! Because we were remembering when we were stuck in the bathroom in the mall. Kacey had stuffed paper towels in the sinks! And overflowed the sinks! And made a flood there, too!!!!

(Well, Jennifer wasn't laughing 'cuz she didn't get the joke. And I didn't want to leave her out. So I told her about Kacey. Then she started cracking up too!!!)

We're all totally laughing. And then ... the bathroom door opened.

Lauren stuck her head in.

Uh oh.

"Girls? WHAT is going on?" She looked around.

"Um," I said. "More Bathroom Bonding?"

She gave us a look. And then shook her head and closed the door.

Yah, that's right ... Bathroom Bonding!

HOLLYWOOD STYLE!!!

# chapter 9

74 sheep. 75 sheep. 76 sheep. Baaaaa.

OK. Lying in bed here. Counting sheep. Not working. Sleep is so not happening for me. I keep thinking about my day. Today was AWESOME!

Jennifer is way sweet. I'm glad we're going to give her a Too Crew bracelet. It will remind her she's got some new friends. It must be hard to go to a new school. To try to start totally new the way she has to. I mean, I've had my friends at school practically forever. I knew who I'd be hanging with next year. Brittany, Haley, Danielle. It would be soooo hard to start over and just make new friends!

But hm. I guess I am not so bad at making new friends, huh?!?! I mean, like Kacey, Isabel, and Claire?! I mean I only met them a couple of weeks ago. And we are all totally friends now so ....

Anyway. I am so not asleep. I can't lie here anymore. Hm.

There was a computer on the desk in the main living room. I could check my e-mail. I turned the computer on.

BWWWINGG!!!!!!

Ack, where's that volume control! Ok, ok, ok ... turned the volume down so I wouldn't wake anyone up.

bwing!

Better.

Sign on ... MaddyBlue.

Yay! I've got mail!

```
From: BrittanyCheer
To: Maddyblue
Subject: Modeling

Hi, Maddy. I can't believe ur in Hollywood
with all those big stars. First modeling
then this huh? don't get a big ego HA HA.

but NE way if ur not 2 busy signing autographs
find out how I can be a model? be4 school
starts. g2g. have to get up early tomorrow
for practice. we have 2 do r new routine
AGAIN. Because Danielle totally can't do it
right. I was like how did you even make the
team if u can't do this easy step! oops no
offense since you didn't even make cheerleading!
cya! Britty
```

OK. Remember when I said it was so great to have the same friends forever? Some days it didn't feel so great! Because OK, I have to say this:

Five years of Brittany was starting to get to me!!!

Because that e-mail made me feel stressed out!!!!

So hey! Maybe my chances of making cheerleading if I tried out WERE:

0% ☹ ———————————— 100%

But did she have to say it like THAT?

See, here's the thing. Brittany can be reallllly fun. And reallllly funny. Like she can imitate practically any teacher at school. Way hilarious! And she always has great ideas for stuff to do. Like when she slept over at my house and put purple nail polish on Zack's toes while he was sleeping. Hee.

But lately ... she was just ... I don't know. Something. Like I didn't see the Super-Fun Brittany as much. Lately, every time the phone rang and it was her ... or I got an e-mail from her ... or was hanging out with her ... I felt ... STRESSED!!!!!!

I wished my BFF Taylor were around. She moved to LA this summer. Yes, LA, where Hollywood is! But she was on a camping trip. In Oregon. A whole other state. BAD timing. I wish I could talk to her about it.

"Pssst ... Hey!"

Oh! Someone whispered behind me. It made me jump! It was Isabel! She was wearing light purple pajamas and had her hair up in a bandanna wrap.

"Sorry, I didn't mean to wake anyone up," I said. "I couldn't sleep."

"Oh, that's OK. I just woke up on my own," she said. "Were you on the computer?"

"Yeah," I told her. "I checked my e-mail. Big mistake, though."

"Why?"

I really didn't want to talk about it. Easier to ignore it.

"You might feel better if you talked about it," Isabel said.

All right, all right. So I told her how I'd gotten that e-mail from Brittany. And once I started talking about it, it all came out in this big rush of words. This is what I said:

"OK. So every time I talk to Brittany, it's way stressful. I'm always worrying I'm going to say something to make her mad! Every time something good happens to me, she gets mad! Like why didn't it happen to her? And she's mean to Danielle! One of our best friends!!!!"

Whew!

I flopped down on the couch. "But anyway, whatever. It's not like I can do anything about it," I finished.

"Oh yeah, you're right," Isabel said, in a sarcastic voice. "You shouldn't do anything about it. Brittany makes you feel stressed out. She gets mad when good things happen to you. And she cuts down your other friend. Um, and you're OK with that?"

Well ...

"Well, she's not like that all the time," I told Isabel. "And usually not so much to me. We've been friends for a long time so I'm used to it."

Isabel looked at me. "Hey, girl, being a loyal friend is one thing," she said carefully. "This doesn't sound cool to me. I don't know. Do you really want to be friends with her? I guess if you do, you'd better do something!"

Uh oh. I don't want to mess with anything.

"Don't worry," Isabel said "I'll think of some ideas. Something to make it better. Not worse."

I didn't know what her advice would be. But somehow I felt a little better already. Isabel always seemed to know the right thing to do. I could think about it tomorrow.

"Thanks, Isabel!" I said. I yawned as she went back to her room. Oh yeah. Maybe I could actually SLEEP now!!! But Oops! Pitch black! Can't see a thing! I started feeling around for my bed. Whoops! I bumped into Kacey's bed.

"GOAL! Yeessssss!"

Wah?!!!! Oh, Kacey was talking in her sleep! Hee hee. Wow! She even dreamed sports.

I found my bed. I grabbed my bear, Pepper, and got under the covers. I pressed Pepper's paw. Taylor had recorded a message to me inside the Build-A-Bear. And the message was: "Maddy, you're a GREAT FRIEND!"

I smiled and closed my eyes. Good night.

# chapter 10

*"Good morning. So nice to see you, dahling. Kiss kiss. Have my people call your people. Must go to the studio now. My limo is waiting."*

That's my Hollywood Star impression. Not bad, huh?

I'd finally fallen asleep last night. And now it was morning! It's ZOE ZONE DAY! We got up early this morning. And pretty much went right to the limo to go to the studio. A big huge super long stretch dealie.

And it had to be a big limo! 'Cuz we were all in it: Kacey, Isabel, Claire, and the Grand Prize Winner, Jennifer. Lauren, my mom, Bruno, and Jennifer's Aunt Dee. Oh— and I almost forgot! ME TOO!

Jennifer was totally Grand Prized up! She was wearing the whole new totally fun outfit she got to pick out as a prize from Limited Too: Shirt, skirt, choker, earrings, bracelet, shoes, bag, and sunglasses! The works!

And ... later on ... she didn't know it yet ... Jennifer would be wearing a charm bracelet, too! Lauren had agreed when Claire asked her! And even got the store to send a bracelet for Jennifer! We were saving it for a surprise.

I couldn't wait to give it to her!

This is what Lauren told us: We're going to be shown around the studio. Jennifer will get to meet Zoe Montana. We don't know when. And it might be quick 'cuz she's busy with TV Star stuff. But she *will* meet ZOE!!!! AND Jennifer will be on the show! She'll be one of the Zoe softball teammates!

Lauren held up a black binder that said "THE ZOE ZONE" on it. COOL! The official script for today's "The Zoe Zone"!

"The script shows the scene you're in, Jennifer," Lauren said.

"The scene I'm in?" Jennifer asked. She looked excited. But she also looked freaked out.

"Yes, you'll be a player on Zoe's softball team," Lauren explained. "And that's when you'll have your close-up."

"My close-up?" Jennifer said. More like, Jennifer squeaked. Pretty cool, huh? Jennifer's going to get a close-up! Here's what the script says!

## MA'S DINER – DAYTIME

TEAM ENTERS WITH ZOE ON THEIR SHOULDERS

**Teammates:**

*Zoe! Zoe! Zoe! Yeahayyyy, Zoe!*

TEAM PUTS ZOE DOWN

**Arthur:**

*Speech! We want a speech from our fearless leader!*

**Zoe:**

*Today was a day of victory! The day we thought would never come! They said our team wouldn't do it. They said our team couldn't do it! Well today we proved them all wrong! And we can always count on each other! We're a true team!*

CLOSE-UP OF **CONTEST WINNER'S** FACE.

TEAM CHEERS. FADE OUT

Jennifer was chewing on her fingernail. She read the script. Over and over again.

"I think Jennifer's really nervous about the whole TV thing," I whispered to Claire, who was sitting next to me in the backward seat of the limo.

"Yes, I think so, too," she whispered back. "She's just so shy! It might be hard for her!"

Isabel noticed, too. "Hey, Jennifer, don't worry. The TV people know what they're doing. They obviously think you can do it. We know you can do it."

"Yeah, Jennifer," I said. "It'll be fun. You'll do a great job." I tried to be reassuring. I mean, I thought she would be fine. She didn't have to say anything. Just go out there and smile! And pretend to cheer!

But Jennifer kept staring at the script. She looked worried. And I mean WAAAAY worried.

"OK, girls!" Lauren said. "We have reached the studio! We're here!!!!!!"

Our limo pulled up to the studio lot, where TV shows and movies and videos are made! Our driver showed his ID at the security gate. We drove in through some roads. We parked and got out of the car ... and right into some historical era thing.

OK! This was SO not "The Zoe Zone." Because we were surrounded by old-fashioned people! This crowd of women in long, poufy skirt things. And a bunch of men wearing big hats. And these weird short pants.

Did we do a TIME WARP? Am I in the 1800's?

"Look, guys! They must be filming a period piece outside," Lauren said. "Look at the intricate costumes. Look at the wonderful hoop skirts on the women and breeches on the men ...."

"And look at Carlo Rossi!" Isabel interrupted, pointing.

WHOA!!!! There, wearing those breeches things and a vest and a fake mustache was CARLO ROSSI! One of the biggest movie stars in the universe!

"Ohmigosh!" Kacey said. "That's really Carlo Rossi! But he looks so 1800's!!!"

Well, besides that he was talking on a cell phone and drinking a cup of coffee.

We stood and looked at him. I tried not to stare. But I mean please! It's a FAMOUS MOVIE STAR! I could try to be all "Oh yeah. SO no big deal. I see famous movies stars everyday ...." Cool like that. But nope! I was going to have to STARE!!!

"OK, girls, time to move on," Lauren said. "We have to get to the set!"

I took one last look at Famous Movie Star Carlo Rossi! And started to follow Lauren away.

But then Lauren turned around and said it again. "Time to move on!"

And then ....

"Excuse me, Pam. We do need to move on. Pam! Pam!"

Um, wait. Pam was my mom's name. And huh? My mom was going in the wrong direction. She was looking all moony ....

And she was totally following Carlo Rossi!

"Pam! Pam Sparks!" Lauren called a little louder. "We need to go this way!"

Oooookay. My mom CLEARLY has this thing for Carlo Rossi!

"Moooooom!" I hissed loudly. "Over here!"

"Oh!" my mom turned around quickly and hurried to catch up with us. She was blushing. "Sorry. I got a little carried away."

"We need to be at Soundstage 9," Lauren said. This time we ALL followed her.

We walked up to the door of a building. Somebody opened the door for me and I walked through it.

"Thank you," I said.

"VELL GIZZPLOWT!" the giant green alien holding the door open for me answered.

ACK!!!!! I grabbed Claire's arm. A giant green alien?!!!

The giant green alien waved its tentacle at me.

"How fun! I heard they were filming Space Battle 2 this month!" Lauren said. "That must be one of the new characters!"

"And he had such nice manners," Claire said, seriously. "Holding the door for you. And I think 'Vell gizzplowt' must mean 'You're welcome.'"

That cracked us all up!

We walked in. We were in a studio! Well, the hallway of one. Lauren said first we would go to the Green Room. That's show biz talk for the room where guests wait till they go on to the set. It wasn't even green, though! It was blue with grey chairs, a couch, and a television monitor. There were posters of "The Zoe Zone" on the walls everywhere. There were also life-size cardboard statue things of Zoe and Arthur! We were entering ... "The Zoe Zone"!!!!

A woman named Anna came into the Green Room. She looked normal. At least she wasn't wearing a hoop skirt! And she wasn't an alien! Her job was production assistant. Today that meant she'd be in charge of us. She gave us the game plan.

**The Game Plan:**

**1. Jennifer would get ready to go on the show. (That meant wardrobe! And makeup! And hair!)**
**2. The Too Crew would hang in the Green Room until she was ready. (The Green Room that's blue!)**

**3. We'd all go on a backstage tour. (ME! Backstage!!)**
**4. Then we'd go watch "The Zoe Zone" getting filmed.
(Starring Jennifer! Go, Jennifer!)**

So first up: Wardrobe! Makeup! Hair!

Oh YEAH. Wardrobe, makeup, hair ... I knew that routine.
I'd been there, done that. Hee hee. OK, just once. When
we were models for the catazine. It was so glam!

My hair had never looked better in my life, I have to tell
you! I was glad I'd have the picture in the catazine as
proof that my hair COULD look good!

"This part is way fun," Isabel told Jennifer. "You're
going to feel like a star. You'll get your clothes for the
show picked out for you. They'll put on makeup, do your
hair all great. Total princess stuff."

"Oh, wow!" Jennifer gasped. Anna and Lauren and Aunt
Dee went off with her.

Have fun being glamorous, Jennifer! The Too Crew also
will be glamorous hanging out in the Green Room of
"The Zoe Zone."

"I can't wait to get to the show! And see Zoe Montana!"
Kacey said, all excited.

I looked at the cardboard statue of Zoe's friend Arthur. And I can't wait to see Arthur, too. I hope I get to see him, too! In real life.

Because Austin Hamilton? He IS #4 on my Ultimate Crush List, you know!!!!

I got up and stood next to Cardboard Arthur.

"How do I look with Arthur?" I asked everyone. I put my arm around him. I patted the blond spiky cardboard hair.

"Awwww, what a cute couple," Isabel said.

"He doesn't talk much," I said. I poked Cardboard Arthur.

Oops! Cardboard Arthur fell over! I put my arms out and caught him. The Cardboard Arthur slid around.

"I think he wants to dance with me," I said. I started to move him around like I was dancing with him.

"I hate to point this out, Maddy. But you're dancing with a piece of cardboard!" Isabel said, laughing.

"Shh!" I told her. "Please don't insult my man. He is an excellent dancer." I danced the Cardboard Arthur around the room.

Everyone was cracking up!

I twirled Cardboard Arthur! I whirled Cardboard Arthur!

"Oh Arthur, you are such a wonderful dancer!" I said loudly. "Arthur, you are soooooo cute!"

And I happened to look out the door at this guy walking past the Green Room. He kinda looked in.

Oops! Busted! Dancing with Cardboard Arthur! But wait a minute .... The guy looked really familiar with his blond hair spiking up and ....

I looked at the guy. I looked at Cardboard Arthur. I looked back at the guy.

OHMIGOSH ... the guy was AUSTIN HAMILTON! The guy who plays Arthur! The guy who is #4 on my Ultimate Crush List!!!!!!

The guy who is ... oh ... walking by as I'm dancing with a cardboard version of him.

*Please don't let him have seen me dancing. Oh please keep walking by because you did not see that I was dancing with a giant piece of cardboard! And telling it how cute it was! Please, please, please!!*

Austin Hamilton kept on walking. WHEW!!!! Saved!

"You GUYS!" I whispered. "Austin Hamilton just walked by the door! The REAL one! Not the cardboard one!"

"Are you serious?!" Kacey squealed. "AUSTIN HAMILTON?!"

"Shhhh!" I said, "He might still be out there!"

Ohmigosh! Ohmigosh! I ran to the door to see. Everyone else ran over, too! We wanted to see AUSTIN HAMILTON! I tried not to seem too obvious peeking out the door. But that was hard to do with Isabel, Claire, and Kacey trying to peek out, too and ...

... knocking me over and right out the door. Knocking me over flat on my face!

Ka-THUNK. Flat on my face right behind Austin Hamilton!!

# chapter 11

So yes, it's true. There I was, face down on the floor. Just me. All alone.

Because Kacey, Isabel, and Claire had jumped back into the Green Room, laughing. But me? I wasn't fast enough.

I was BUSTED.

**Red-face Rating:** ★★★☆ out of ★★★★★ stars. *Um, Hello #4 on my Ultimate Crush List! From face down on the FLOOR.*

"Hey! Girl on the Floor! You all right?" Austin Hamilton said, walking back over.

And what did I say back to him?

> a) Yes, I'm fine, thank you. It's very nice to meet you. I am a great admirer of your work.
> b) Yes, no problem. I am a professional stunt woman just practicing my next scene.
> c) Yeah, thanks.
> d) Glak.

The answer was "d."

OK, OK, OK! I know, I know! Glak?!!! What's up with me saying "GLAK"?!!???! That's even worse than "GAH"! But tell me what you think YOU'D have said. If you were suddenly, unexpectedly, lying flat on your face in front of #4 on your Ultimate Crush List who is also a big TV star?!!!!!!!!!!

I can't believe I said "GLAK."

Fortunately Austin seemed to understand Crazy Wacko Fan Speak.

"Good, you're not hurt. Let me help you up," he said, holding out his hand to help me up. I reached out and grabbed his hand ....

YES, I TOUCHED AUSTIN HAMILTON'S HAND. IT'S TRUE, I REALLY DID!!!!!

"Be careful, okay?" he told me. He smiled and started walking away.

Buh-bye, Austin Hamilton. Big TV Star. #4 Crush-o-rama. And, oh yeah. He was waaaay cute in person. Forget #4. I'm thinking we have a contender for the #3 position on my list. Maybe #2 even!

Austin Hamilton is **MOVING ON UP!!!!**

Then Kacey, Isabel, and Claire peeked out the door. Just in time to see Austin Hamilton turn around. And hear him say to me:

"Oh, Girl on the Floor? Sorry I interrupted your dance!"

ACK!!!!!!!!!!!!!! ACK!!!!!!!!!!!!!!!

I ran back into the Room. Kacey, Isabel, and Claire were lying all over the couches. And laughing!

ACK!!!!!!!!

"I can't believe Austin Hamilton saw me dancing with his Cardboard Self!" I shrieked. "That is the most embarrassing thing ever!!!!!!"

"Actually, what would be more embarrassing is if he heard you telling the piece of cardboard how cute it was," Isabel said.

"OH NO! He probably did that, too!" I groaned. ACK!!!!!!!!

Now Kacey, Isabel, and Claire were laughing HARD. Reallllllly hard. Like holding their sides laughing! Like rolling around on the couch laughing!!!

Okay, it is pretty hilarious. If it ISN'T HAPPENING TO YOU.

I walked over to Cardboard Arthur.

"We are so OVER!" I said. I knocked him against the wall.

"Maddy!" Isabel stopped laughing. "Do you realize Austin Hamilton touched your hand?!"

OH! IT'S TRUE! OK. Yes, I was totally humiliated! Yes, I was totally embarrassed! But YES! Austin Hamilton, TV star, touched my hand when he helped me up!!!

Everyone gathered around me to check out my hand. My right hand. Yes, the hand that Austin Hamilton touched. My hand. Mine ... mine ... MINE!

I felt better now!!!!

"That was nice of him to help you up," Claire said. "He has nice manners." Claire was very polite. She noticed things like that. I have to say I was more noticing his

**GORGEOUS BLUE EYES!**

But yeah, he was so nice! He's a big huge star being nice to me, me, ME!!!

We were all still admiring my hand when a woman and a girl around our age walked into the Green Room.

"Hey, isn't that —?" I started to whisper to Kacey. It was! The girl was the actress who played Megan, Zoe's awesome teammate and best friend at school.

"Hi, girls," the woman said. "This is Tiffany Tyler, who plays Megan on the show. I'm her manager. And also her mother. We wanted to congratulate you on winning the contest."

"Hi, it's nice to meet you," Isabel said. "But actually, the contest winner is in wardrobe right now. We're just the helpers."

Tiffany Tyler rolled her eyes and gave us a dirty look.

"Well, thanks for wasting my time," she said to her manager-also-her-mother. And she was not quiet about it! "They aren't anybody!" Tiffany stomped out of the room. Her mother followed her out.

Yow.

"Wow," Claire said. "That wasn't very polite."

"She reminds me of ..." I said. And Kacey and I said it at the same time:

"PIPER!"

Yes, Piper! One of the models from the catazine shoot. She'd been pretty rude to us, too.

"And just as we did with Piper, we will ignore this Tiffany girl's attitude," Isabel said. "Who needs it?!"

Yeah, who needs it? Yeah! YEAH! Isabel was so cool! Isabel didn't let anyone bother her! Without Isabel around, I probably would have been like, "Did I do something wrong? Did I say something wrong?" But nope, it wasn't me! Tiffany was just plain R-U-D-E!

"Did you see the way she treated her mother?" Claire said, frowning. "That was awful."

"Well, I hope my mom meets Tiffany and then appreciates me," I said. Everyone smiled.

Except for Kacey. Hmmm. Something weird was going on. Kacey actually looked ...

SAD. Not her usual happy self. She wasn't bouncing around all happy! She was sitting there looking ... well, bummed out. Kacey! If I hadn't seen it, I wouldn't have believed it! That she got bummed out even for one second.

"Kacey, is something wrong?" I asked her. "You look bummed. Did that Tiffany girl get to you?"

"Oh, ugh, no way," Kacey said. "I was just, well, all of a sudden when you were talking about mothers, I started missing my mom. Maybe I sound like a baby, but I really miss my mom. And my dad. And my sister, Emily."

Kacey, happy happy Kacey, looked so sad. I felt so bad for her. I didn't know what to do. I looked at Isabel, like, "What should we do?" But before she could do anything, Claire spoke up.

"Kacey! That's not babyish. Why don't you call home?" she asked. "Use my cell phone. I really do have a ton of free minutes, so go ahead and talk all you want to. Isabel, Maddy, feel free to use it, too."

Kacey smiled through her tears. She reached over and gave Claire a hug. She had a smile on her face again as she took the phone and walked just outside the room.

"Excuse me for a moment," Claire said. "I need to go to the girls' room," Claire said, pointing to a door.

"If we don't hear from you in ten minutes we'll come break the door down!" Isabel told her. It was our inside joke! From being stuck in the bathroom together!

Isabel turned to me. "So Maddy. Seeing that snotty girl reminds me of something. The sitch with your friend,

Brittany. And how she treats you."

Oh. Uh. Do we really have to think about THAT?

"You know what? I think it will all be OK!" I told her.
Let's move on! I started chewing on my hair. Chew.
Chew. Chew.

"Come on, Maddy. Wouldn't you feel so much better if
you didn't have to stress about her?" Isabel asked.
"Honestly?"

OK, honestly, yeah. Sure. But I was feeling stressed out
NOW thinking of actually doing something about it.
Chew. Chew. Chew.

"OK. Here's what I'm thinking," Isabel said. "You COULD
just be like, SEE YA, BRITTANY! And go find some new
friends, you know. But you said a lot of the time she IS
a pretty good friend. So you want to give it a try and
save the friendship, first?"

I nodded.

"All right. Here's what I think you should do, Maddy. You
should talk to Brittany about how you're feeling."

"I can't!" I burst out. "She'll get mad at me!!!"

"Yeah, probably," Isabel agreed. "Especially at first. But I mean, hey. Like my sister Jessica always says, friends are honest with each other. If you don't talk to her, things aren't gonna change. They'll just get worse."

Worse?!!! I don't want THAT to happen.

Isabel was like this walking advice column. I had to admit, she'd always pretty much been right in the past. And she sounded right on this, too. But say something to Brittany? I have to SAY something to Brittany?

"OK," I said, feeling kind of sickish to my stomach about it. "Fine. I'll talk to her when I get back home. But I don't know what I'll say to her."

Kacey bounced back into the Green Room. She had a big smile on her face again. Yeah! "My mom says 'hi'!" she said. "And so does Emily. Hey, where's Claire?"

"She's in the bathroom," I told her.

"By herself? A girl can't go to the bathroom alone," Kacey giggled. "Actually, I'd better go too! Wash my face! I probably look all 'crying' and stuff. I'll be back in a couple of minutes." She put the cell phone on an empty seat.

"You know what," Isabel said, eying the phone. "It might

be better to talk to Brittany in person. BUT if you want my help with it, it might not be a bad idea to call Brittany now. Claire said she had free minutes you could use on her phone."

Gulp. Isabel was right. I really SHOULD be able to talk to Brittany about this. She's my friend and friends can do that, right? Right? And it might be easier with Isabel here to watch my back.

Gulp. Then why was I so nervous? I chewed my hair faster. Chew. Chew. CHOMP! But ....

"Okay, I'll do it."

I picked up the cell phone.

# chapter 12

I was going to do it. I was going to make the call. I was going to talk to Brittany! And ... um ....

"What am I supposed to say?" I asked Isabel.

Isabel told me the plan.

So I dialed Brittany's house. I sent thought waves to Ohio. Don't be home, don't be home, PLEASE don't be home! Be at the mall ... Be at cheerleading ... Be fast asleep dreaming about cheerleading so you can't hear the phone ring.

"Hello?"

Rats.

"Hi, Brittany," I said into the phone. "It's Maddy. You busy?"

"Hey, Maddy," I heard Brittany say from thousands of miles away. "I'm working on some posters for basketball cheerleading tryouts. Oh, sorry! Touchy subject with you, huh? Hey, are you calling me from LA? Did you meet any stars yet or what?"

I told her about meeting Austin. Brittany was quiet for a minute.

"Well, Austin Hamilton. That's not so big a deal. I met bigger stars than that before," Brittany said. "But anyway. Pretty soon I guess you'll be back here with the regular people, with things back to normal. Watching us do our cheerleading and stuff. We'll try not to forget you next time and leave you off the bus. Ha ha. JUST KIDDING!"

Oooookay. Even thousands of miles away, in two seconds, I'm reminded why I am making this call. I looked at Isabel. She gave me the thumbs up. Yes. OK. Deep breath.

"Um, Brittany," I said. "I wanted to talk to you a minute. About something that's sorta important to me. You know we've been friends a long time. And ya know you're really special to me. But ...."

Well ... here goes.

"I've been feeling kinda bad about some of the things you've been saying. Like when you make fun of me for not making cheerleading. And make fun of Danielle for not being good when she's cheerleading ...."

"Oh puh-lease, Maddy. You know I'm only kidding." Brittany laughed a little. "Don't be so sensitive. Lighten up. We're going to be in a new school this year! It's going to be brutal. If you can't take a little kidding around from one of your best friends, I mean, get real. You'll never survive."

"Um, Brittany?" I said. "Maybe you think you're kidding, but it makes me really feel bad. And I'm nervous enough about starting this new school. I mean, I'm bummed about not making cheerleading. I really need my friends, like you, to support me. Not to make me feel bad."

There was silence on the other line. Then Brittany spoke.

"OK, whatEVER, Maddy," Brittany said. "Have fun in Hollywood. Buh-bye." Click.

**Q&A:**

**Q:** What would be the worst sound you could hear on the phone after confronting Brittany?
**A:** CLICK. Which means Brittany hung up on me. Which means she has dismissed me. Done. Over. Buh-Bye.

Ohmigosh. Oh no.

"Isabel!!!" I called. "I think I really screwed up. Brittany just totally hung up on me!!!! She's really mad!"

OK, I was FREAKING out. BRITTANY JUST HUNG UP ON ME!!!!

"All right, all right," Isabel said. "Relax a sec. Did you say what we planned out?"

I nodded.

"Then you were just sticking up for yourself and you needed to," she continued. "You said what you had to say."

"But if I didn't say it, she wouldn't be mad at me!" I said. "Now she's going to come after me or something!"

"Hey listen," Isabel continued. "If she does something mean because you were honest, she's not really a friend, right? You said you thought she was a good friend. Let's see if she can prove it. 'Cuz just because you've had a friend for a long time doesn't mean you should stay friends forever!"

My heart was still pounding. I knew Isabel was right! But I was going to be the one who had to deal with the consequences! I mean, I couldn't believe I had just said that to Brittany. And she had hung up on me. Was I going to be in major trouble when I got back or what?!!!!!

BUZZZZZZZZ. My head felt all buzzy. RINGGGGGG. My ears started ringing. Oh wait, that wasn't my ears. That was Claire's cell phone.

"Hello?" I said.

"Maddy?" this voice said on the other end of the line. "It's me, Brittany. I caller ID'd you back. I guess I shouldn't have hung up on you. And, uh, I guess I should explain some stuff ...."

**This Journal Belongs to:**

Maddy Elizabeth Sparks

WEIRD WEIRD WEIRD! OK, so this is what happened. I was totally FREAKING OUT! I mean Brittany hung up on my face! I thought maybe she'd never talk to me again!!!!

But she called me back. And said stuff like...

She's stressed out about starting our new school,

too. And sorta jealous of me and the stuff I was getting to do like the catazine and stuff! So, yeah, maybe she was being a little harsh.

And she said she was SORRY she had hurt my feelings!!!! CAN YOU EVEN BELIEVE IT??? Ohmigosh!!! She really sounded like she meant it!!!!!!!!

So I did the next thing Isabel had told me to do. I told Brittany it was OK and, thanks for saying she was sorry. But could she please stop doing all that stuff from now on? Because like, that's not what friends do!!!!!!!!

And I told her I wanted to help her out with her dream of being a model. So I told her what I knew: At the catalog shoot, some of the other models got their jobs through these places called talent agencies.

Then I told her the name of the agency we remembered Piper mentioning. Isabel told me this talent agency is good. Because that's where Limited Too got some of its models.

So I tried to help her out. And she said, "Thanks." Wow. Brittany told me she was sorry AND she thanked me. **UNBELIEVABLE!**

Oh, but then she goes, "OK I have to finish the posters for Basketball Cheerleading tryouts." I asked her what the dates were and she goes, "Oh Maddy, the same girls who made football can try out for basketball, you know. So it's not like it's going to be any easier for you to make it or anything. So guess you'd better just skip it."

So, well. Not a whole lot of support at the end, there. She's STILL Brittany. But I had told her how I felt. And now I will wait and see! Maybe our friendship will be better. I hope so!!!!! Anyway, I feel SOOO MUCH BETTER NOW!!!!

Kacey and Claire came back in the room. "Guess what!" Kacey said. "I just saw Jennifer coming down the hall!"

Back from Makeup! Hair! And Wardrobe! To get ready for ... "THE ZOE ZONE"!!

# chapter 13

Jennifer looked SERIOUSLY amazing. She was wearing a white and blue softball uniform that said "Ma's Diner" on it. She was wearing a softball hat. Her makeup looked really cute. But what totally made her look great was this huge gigundo smile! Not her usual shy smile, but like a huge glowy one!

"You look awesome!" Kacey told her. "Totally Zoe Zone!"

Lauren told us the deal:

⭐ Maddy's mom, Bruno, and Jennifer's Aunt Dee will wait in the Green Room and watch everything on the monitors.
⭐ The Too Crew gets to see the action close up! We get to go right to the set!!!!!!

SWEET!!!!!!!

So this is how it worked. Anna came in and told us to follow her to Soundstage 9. We left the front area and went down a hall. She opened a big door and we went into a huge room with really high ceilings. It was cold in there and smelled kind of dusty. There was stuff piled everywhere.

"Are we in the right place?" Claire whispered to me. I was thinking the same thing. It was quiet and empty and dark and freezing and ... OH!

LOOK! There was Zoe's living room! And Zoe's classroom! Well, they looked like a living room and classroom. But they were really just the furniture and stuff. With really thin walls set up to look like rooms.

"These are all sets we use on 'The Zoe Zone,'" Anna explained. "Today we're shooting on the diner set, so they're empty. You might recognize them from the show."

I did! Even the little stuff. Like the fake fish tank and the clock hanging on the fake wall. I saw that stuff on "The Zoe Zone"!!!

"It seems so much smaller," Kacey said. "It all looks so much bigger on TV."

"Yes, that's true," Anna said. "The cameras give everything depth and make it seem much larger when you watch it. There are lots of tricks."

"You've probably seen Zoe and her team hang out at Ma's Diner after their games," Anna said, as we followed her. "Well, that's where we're shooting. And here it is.

Right over here ...."

And then I saw it. MA'S DINER! There it was! Exactly like on TV! The red and white tables, the jukeboxes on the tables, the counter. Exactly! Well, except that there were people pushing around cameras on wheels and holding lights and giant microphones. There were people racing around everywhere!

Anna told us who some of the people were:

- ★ The director, who's in charge of making sure everyone does what they need to do.
- ★ A couple of assistant directors to help out the director.
- ★ Camera people, lighting people, and sound people.
- ★ The makeup and hair people, for touch-ups.
- ★ And of course ... the actors.

"Wow, look at all that food!" Kacey pointed to a long buffet table. It had tons of food all over it.

"You'll get a chance to hit the buffet later," Anna said to us. "Right now, I think we're almost ready to go on set!"

On set! Going on set at "The Zoe Zone"!!!!!

"Ohmigosh," Jennifer breathed.

There's Austin Hamilton walking on to the set!

AUSTIN!!!

(Did I mention Austin Hamilton touched my hand?)

AND OHMIGOSH! ZOE MONTANA WAS WALKING ON THE SET!!! I WAS IN THE SAME ROOM AS ZOE MONTANA! She's right in front of my own face!

We were all like AHHHHHHHHHHHHHH!

Especially Jennifer! She was like AHHHHHHHHHHHH! ZOE MONTANA!!!!

"Time to go on set!" Anna came over to Jennifer.

"I'm going to go up there? By Zoe Montana?!!!!" Jennifer said. She was like EEK!

Isabel gave her a smile. Kacey gave her a high five. Claire gave her a little hug. I said, "Good luck, Jennifer!!!!"

Anna brought Jennifer on the set. She was supposed to stand with a group of actors. They were all softballed up in their uniforms.

Jennifer was standing next to that Tiffany Tyler. Bluch.

Hope Tiffany doesn't say anything mean.

OK! It was SHOW TIME!

"Take one! Action!" the director person called. YEAH! ACTION! GO JENNIFER!!!!

The team carried Zoe in on their shoulders. Like in the script!!!! They were all pretending to cheer and be all excited. They put Zoe down and then Arthur spoke: "Speech! We want a speech from our fearless leader!" Then Zoe started her speech: "Today was a day of victory! The — ...."

"CUT!" The director yelled all of a sudden. "What's going on with the Extra?!!!"

Because Jennifer, our contest winner, was sneaking off the set.

"What's she doing?" I whispered to Isabel. She looked at me like UH OH! Anna ran over to Jennifer. She started talking to her.

Tiffany made a snorty sound and rolled her eyes like, "What a loser."

"Oh no!" Claire said. "Jennifer's so shy! She must be panicking!"

Oh noooooooooo ...!

"Come on," Isabel said. "Let's go see if we can help. I mean, that's what we're here for, right?"

We ran over to the side of the set. Jennifer was standing with Anna and Lauren. Jennifer was crying.

"She says she's too nervous for her close-up," Lauren explained to us.

"I can't do it!" Jennifer said. "I'll look all 'DUH' or something. I know I'll screw it up!"

Oh, I'd been there before. I knew how she was feeling.

"Just try it, Jennifer," Isabel said. "We know you can do it!"

"Go, Jennifer, go!" Kacey cheered. "You're so perfect to be on Zoe's team!"

"When I get panicky, I take some deep breaths. I imagine I'm somewhere safe and relaxing," Claire said. That was the advice Isabel had given her in the bathroom on the day we met.

Jennifer took some deep breaths, but still looked shaky.

"Jennifer, I totally know what you're going through." I quickly told her about:

- ★ How I almost didn't even show up for the first day of the catazine shoot. Because I'd been soooo nervous I'd screw it up!
- ★ How I ended up falling during the shoot and knocking everyone over. Totally embarrassing. But then it all worked out great.
- ★ How, ok, I was always embarrassing myself! But, I'd learned I had to just give things a try anyway.

"So," I told her. "If it makes you feel better, I'm pretty much used to embarrassing myself. You just gotta stop thinking about it. You'll be bummed out forever if you don't get out there!!!!! You'll be like, 'I missed my chance.'"

The director yelled, "Everybody! Places, everyone! Contest winner? Are you IN? Or are you OUT?!"

Jennifer sniffed. She looked at us. Kacey, Isabel, Claire and I gave her thumbs up. Jennifer went back over to where the team was standing. Super quick, the makeup artist ran over and did some stuff to Jennifer's eyes where the makeup had smudged.

"I hope she can do this!" Claire whispered to me.

Do it, Jennifer. Do it, Jennifer. You can do it.

"ACTION!" The Director called out.

Take 2

The team carried Zoe out on their shoulders. Arthur spoke: "Speech! We want a speech from our fearless leader!" Zoe started her speech: "Today was a day of victory!"

Oh no. Jennifer's face STILL looked all scared. She was not looking like the excited teammate! She was standing there all frozen.

What if the director yelled "CUT" again! What if he wouldn't let her do the scene!

"She's freaking!" Kacey whispered. "She's not going to do it. What can we do?"

"Maddy," Isabel looked at me. "You've got to do it. For Jennifer. Take one for the team. Come on."

HUH? Do what?!!!

Kacey ran over to the food table. To a bowl of fruit. Huh? What was going on?!?!! Kacey grabbed a banana and ran it over to me and ....

OHHHHHHHHH!

MONKEY GIRL! Jennifer needed MONKEY GIRL!

OH!!!! Ohhhhkay. Ohhhhh boy. Ohhhhh ... embarrassing.

But OK. I knew what I had to do. I stepped forward, where Jennifer could see me.

Jump. Jump. Jump.

I started to jump up and down. I could see Jennifer looking over at me. She was all: What's going on??? What's Maddy DOING???

Yes. Fine. I felt like a total DORK! But I kept going.

I scratched under my arms. I scratched my head. Jennifer looked at me like I was nuts. I could see some of the cast looking at me, too. Zoe continued on with her speech. I started jumping around, scratching. Doing some serious monkey stuff. Now half the crew was looking at me like I was nuts.

Jump! Scratch! Monkey Stuff!

I held up the banana. And then ....

Jennifer Got It.

"Monkey Girl!" you could see her whisper. And she started to smile. And start to laugh. And START TO CHEER! WITH THE REST OF ZOE'S TEAM!!!!!!!!!!

And the cameras kept rolling!!!! And Zoe kept talking!!!! "Well today we proved them all wrong! And we can always count on each other! We're a true team!"

CLOSE-UP ON CONTEST WINNER'S FACE.

TEAM CHEERS.

YAY ZOE! YAY TEAM! YAY JENNIFER!!!!!!!!! JENNIFER WAS SMILING AND CHEERING WITH THE REST OF THE TEAM! SHE WAS DOING IT!!!

"Cut!" The director said. "Good job, everybody!"

SHE DID IT! Jennifer DID IT! WOO HOO! GO JENNIFER!!!

Even though the scene was over, Kacey, Isabel, and I were still cheering like crazy. Jennifer was smiling like crazy.

And the director turned to me and looked at me like I was crazy.

"What was that all about?" he called over.

To me.

Uhhhhhhh ... How do I explain the monkey thing?

"You know what? I don't want to know," the director said, waving it off. "But I think I need to put that acting ability to use. I need a few extra people to fill in a scene. So Girl Who Acts like a Monkey! You and your friends there want to be on TV? Makeup! Hair! Prep those four girls right there."

OK, HUH?!?!!

I looked at the set. Jennifer was jumping up and down. All smiley! And waving to us like, "Come on!!"

Kacey, Isabel, Claire and I all looked at each other like, "Whaaaaaaaaaaat?!!!" And then Isabel said, "We are soooo ..."

**"HOLLYWOOD!!!!"** we screamed.

WE'RE GOING TO BE ON TV!!!!

And the makeup people ran over to powder and lipstick us! The hair people ran over to brush, fluff, and spray us! Ohmigosh!!!! In like three seconds, we were on the set!!!

"Okay, set up the four new extras!" the director called out. Anna brought us over to one of the diner booths and told us to sit. Some crew brought over plates of food to make it look like we were eating at the diner.

Anna gave us the directions:

"You guys are going to pretend you're just hanging out in the diner. You'll just be in the background while Zoe and Arthur are talking up front. Now, you're going to pretend you're talking to each other and eating your food. BUT you can't make a sound. Or it would interfere with the microphones on Zoe and Arthur. So just move your lips like this.

And she goes, "Mmwah mwah mwah ...." But no sound came out!

"Ready? Roll em!" the director called out.

Whoa. This was too unreal. First of all, Kacey, Isabel, Claire, and I are sitting in the pretend Ma's Diner. Pretending to eat. Pretending we're talking to each other. Mouthing the words with no sound! While Zoe and Arthur are saying their lines.

Hello? Hello?!!!

I WAS ON SET AT "THE ZOE ZONE" BEING FILMED TO BE ON TELEVISION!!!! SITTING BY ZOE MONTANA AND AUSTIN HAMILTON! ME!!!! MADDY ELIZABETH SPARKS! And Kacey. And Isabel. And Claire!!!

MWAH MWAH MWAH! Me and Kacey, and Isabel, and Claire were all pretending to talk to each other. Just moving our lips. Mwah! Mwah? Mwah mwah. Like we're just eating at a diner all normal. Heh heh. Except this was way NOT normal! But it was fun! Mwah mwah! MWAH!

"Cut!" the director called out. "Nice work, everybody! And that's a wrap!"

FADE OUT.

# chapter 14

As soon as the director said, "That's a wrap," everyone took off. The actors! The crew! It was just Anna, Lauren, Jennifer, and the Too Crew left!

"Hey!" Kacey said. "Where'd everyone go?"

"They all have to go get ready for the next scene," Anna said. "They have to keep things moving!"

"Jennifer!" Lauren said. "You did a great job today! I'm so proud of you!"

"I can't believe it's true! I'm going to be on 'The Zoe Zone,'" Jennifer said, all excited. "And I saw Zoe Montana!"

And then I saw Zoe Montana.

No, I mean REALLY saw her. Like, in the room! Zoe Montana was walking across the room toward us, with a woman!!!! She was still wearing the softball uniform she had on in her scene. She's coming closer ... Closer ... Right up to us ....

ZOE MONTANA!!!!!!! COMING OVER TO SEE US!!!

# HOW COOL IS THAT?!!

"Ohmigosh," Jennifer was saying. "Ohmigosh, ohmigosh." Kacey was bouncing around. Claire, and Isabel, and I just had our mouths open.

"Girls, meet Zoe Montana and her manager," Lauren said. "And Zoe, I'd like you to meet Jennifer. She's the Grand Prize Winner of 'The Zoe Zone' contest, and she's here from Arizona."

"Hi, Jennifer!" Zoe said.

Jennifer was like WHOA!!!! She said HI TO ME!!!

"And these four girls are here to help out with the contest," Lauren said. "This is Kacey, Isabel, Claire, and Maddy."

We all said, "Hi!" Hi to the real live and in person Zoe Montana!

"We all love your show!" Kacey spoke up. "Jennifer and I are especially huge fans of yours. I love all sports and Jennifer is really into basketball. Right, Jennifer?"

Jennifer nodded.

"Yes!" she squeaked.

"Cool! You know, you guys are probably better athletes than I am," Zoe said. "I'm not as great at sports in real life as I am on TV. But maybe that means I'm a good actor since I can fake it, right?"

Zoe laughed. Jennifer looked like AAAAH! You could tell she couldn't believe she was meeting her idol. She was smiling!

"Do you girls want to have your picture taken with Zoe?" the manager asked. "She has just about another minute."

A picture with Zoe! A picture with Zoe! Picture Time!

Zoe & Jennifer!

Zoe & Jennifer & her aunt!

Zoe & The Too Crew & Jennifer!

CLICK! — Captured forever on film together!!!!

"Jennifer," Zoe said, when we were done with pictures. "I've gotta go get ready now for my next scene. Thanks again for being on my team!"

"Um, Zoe?" Jennifer said, shyly. "I just wanted to say ...

I mean, I watch you on TV ... and um ... um ... I think you're AWESOME!"

"Oh, THANKS!" Zoe said. "You're so sweet!!!"

And then Zoe Montana waved. And walked away.

"Ohmigosh!" Jennifer said. "Ohmigosh!"

"Okay, Jennifer," Isabel said. "You just met Zoe Montana! You got your picture taken with Zoe Montana! AND she told you that you're sweet!!!"

I WAS SOOOOO HAPPY FOR HER! And for ME!

Maddy's Celebrity Spotting Checklist:

✓ Skyler Hope
✓ Justice, "America's Favorite Teen Super Star"
✓ Carlo Rossi
✓ Austin Hamilton
✓ Tiffany Tyler
✓ Zoe Montana
✓ The weather guy from Channel 5

"I just want to say something, you guys," Jennifer said in her quiet voice. "Thank you soooo much. I know I wouldn't have been able to have done all that if you guys hadn't been there!"

Awwww!!!

"Especially you, Maddy. That monkey thing made me laugh. And I even forgot to be shy!"

"I can't wait to see it on TV!" Kacey said. "Jennifer, think about it. You'll be in Arizona. With all your new basketball teammates. And then be like, "Hey! That's me on 'The Zoe Zone.'"

"This was the best day of my life," Jennifer said. "The best day EVER!"

"And maybe I can make it even better!"

A voice came from behind me. I turned around.

IT WAS AUSTIN HAMILTON!!! WALKING RIGHT OVER TO US!!!

He had a shirt in his hands. He tossed it to Jennifer. Oh COOL! It was the team uniform jersey they'd worn on the show today!!!

"This is to say thanks for coming on the show today. And for being such a big fan," he said. "It's signed by the cast. Just for you."

Jennifer pointed to the front of the shirt. "Ohmigosh! There's Zoe's autograph! For me!!!"

"Yeah! And mine, too, don't forget," he teased. "And for the rest of you, I have some 8 x 10 glossies of the cast."

COOL!!!!!

He held up some big black and white pictures. He took out a black pen and started signing them:

*austin Hamilton - Arthur*

"Thanks, Austin. That's nice of you," Claire said.

"Hey, no prob." He gave Kacey a picture. And Isabel a picture. And Claire. And then he turned to me.

"Hey, I know you. You're like, the girl with many talents," he said to me.

???????!!!!!

"I saw you do the whole monkey thing," Austin said. "That was some acting. The whole thing with my Cardboard Arthur? That was some dancing! And the way you fell on your face, that's like a professional stuntwoman!"

OK. How embarrassing is THAT?!!!

"See you guys later!"

!!!!!!!!!!!

"Maddy, Austin Hamilton remembered you!!!" Kacey squealed.

"Um, acting like a monkey? Dancing with cardboard? Falling on my face? You guys!!!!" I wailed. That's not exactly how I want to be remembered by #3 on my Ultimate Crush List!

ACK!!!!!!!!!!!!

OK. Isabel is cracking up. Kacey? Giggling. Claire? Laughing. Jennifer? That big huge smile thing.

OK OK OK!!! IT IS FUNNY!!!!!!

I was laughing, too!

"Ow, my stomach hurts," Kacey said. "From all this laughing!!!! This whole trip!!"

"You guys are really funny," Jennifer said. "I hope I make some friends in Arizona. Like you."

She held up the shirt Austin had given to her.

"Would you guys sign my jersey too?" Jennifer asked.

"You want us to sign your jersey? The one the cast autographed?" Isabel asked her.

"Yes," Jennifer said shyly. "I mean, you guys were part of the cast today, too. And you guys are like, my friends."

I picked up the pen Austin had left on the table and handed it to Kacey. Who signed and passed it to Isabel. Who signed and passed it to Claire. Who passed it back to me.

Claire Isabel Kacey Maddy!!!

Claire looked over at the three of us. We nodded. It was time.

"And Jennifer, we have something for you," Claire said. She pulled a little box out of her bag. She gave it to Jennifer. Jennifer opened it up.

"A charm bracelet! Just like you guys have!" she breathed.

"We want to say this," I said. "We're happy you've become part of the Too Crew. And when you wear the bracelet, you can always think of how you were a star on 'The Zoe Zone.'"

Jennifer put her bracelet on. And touched the tiny star charm. And you could just tell she felt really special. And she smiled that big, huge smile. ☺

# chapter 15

I held up my right hand for the gazillionth time.

"Does anyone want to see the hand Austin Hamilton touched? Anyone? Anyone?"

Everybody groaned. Ok, ok, enough! They'd seen the hand! Hee.

We were riding back to the hotel in the limo. Jennifer and her aunt had taken another one to the airport. They had to go back to Arizona.

"How cool was it to see Jennifer's face when she opened the box and saw the charm bracelet?" Isabel said.

I was so glad we'd decided to give her a Too Crew bracelet.

"On that note," Lauren turned around from the seat in front of us. She was sitting next to my mom. "I'd like to give you girls something else to remember the day by. A new charm for your charm bracelets. This charm will represent the day you all came to Hollywood. On your very first trip together. But maybe not your last."

Lauren handed us each a little box. We opened them.

"A tiny star like Jennifer's!" I said. I looked closely at the charm. "But look! Mine says Maddy on it!"

"They each have your names on them," Lauren said. "They're supposed to look like a star on the Hollywood Walk of Fame. To remind you of the day you were all superstars on TV. And as friends to Jennifer."

"A star on the Walk of Fame!" Kacey said. "That's cool!"

"Oh yeah! We are sooooo ..." I started the sentence. And we all finished it together:

## HOLLYWOOD!!!

We all took off our charm bracelets and fastened the new charms on them. I looked at mine. It was so cool.

"And that's not all," Lauren said. "I have something else for your memories. It's a copy of the design of the catazine cover. It's going to be mailed out in a few weeks. The one starring all of you ... the Too Crew."

Lauren handed Isabel a glossy sheet of paper. It said Limited Too in blue letters. And there we were. A giant picture of Kacey, Isabel, Claire, and me. We were all in this jumbled pile on the ground. Laughing and smiling.

Ohmigosh. This. Is. So. Cool.

And. We. Look. So. CUTE!!!!

"AHHHHHH!" we all screamed. We were really on the cover of the catazine!!!

I remembered back to that day. Like I'd told Jennifer, I really thought I had screwed up the photo shoot. I remember wondering why I had even bothered to come! Thinking I couldn't do anything right. Ever. And then look what happened. I GOT TO BE ON THE COVER OF A CATAZINE!!!!!

And, um, I'm lookin' pretty good. ME!!!! Heh.

"Girls," Lauren spoke. "You guys should be proud of yourselves. You worked together to help Jennifer out. You guys are a great team. It really meant a lot to Jennifer to have you all there to support her. And the monkey thing, well, really helped out. Maddy, you're a real trooper."

"Speech!" Kacey shouted. "We want a speech from our fearless leader! Maddy! Maddy! Maddy!"

Oh! Arthur's lines in the script! OK! I'm not fearless! I'm not our leader! But that's my cue!

"Today was a day of victory!" I said, in my best Zoe voice. "The day we thought would never come! They said our team wouldn't do it. They said our team couldn't do it! Well today we proved them all wrong! Because ...

We can always count on each other! We really ARE a true team!"

I looked at Kacey, and Isabel, and Claire. They were sooooooo great. We had such an AWESOME time in Hollywood. I couldn't wait to find out what the Too Crew would be doing next!

**Happy Face Rating:**

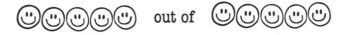 out of

the end ... for now that is! So ...

Stay tuned!

# the
# too crew's
## stuff for
## you to do

# Q&A with Maddy

OK, here's a **Q** for me to **A**. I'll see what I can do ....

**Q:** Dear Maddy: I have a friend kinda like Brittany!!! She's always teasing me and then says, "JUST KIDDING!" How can I tell if it's like nice kidding or nasty kidding!

**A:** Yeah, that is a weird thing. It's like teasing can be good or bad. Like, when Isabel calls me Monkey Girl, that's funny. When Brittany tells me I'm going to be left off the bus, not funny. How do you tell the difference?

Good Q. Here's what I've found out!!!

Teasing: The Good Kind (like Isabel)
- Makes you feel good
- Makes you feel like the person likes you
- You feel like you can ask the person to stop and it's no big deal
- If you ask the person to stop, the person stops
- The person doesn't act like you can't take a joke. Like they don't go "Hey, I'm JUST KIDDING!"

Teasing: The Not So Good Kind (like Brittany)
- The person does it to put you down
- The person doesn't care if it bugs you
- The person acts like something's wrong with you if you don't like it
- You feel like, if you ask the person to stop, they'll get mad or make fun of you or something

# Make a Wish!

Hey, it's me, Maddy! I'm always making Wish Lists of things I want to come true!

Ok, I got to meet some famous people on this trip! How cool is that? But before I went to Hollywood with the Too Crew, I only DREAMED of meeting a real, live celebrity! So I had a Celebrity Spotting Wish List. Celebrities I wanted to meet!

And remember how I have a list of places I dream about going? (Including HOLLYWOOD?!!) I have a Travel Wish List!

Well what's on YOUR Wish Lists?!?!!

**Who's on YOUR CELEBRITY SPOTTING WISH LIST?**

_____

_____

_____

_____

**What are places YOU'd put on your TRAVEL WISH LIST?**

_____

_____

_____

_____

**This Journal Belongs to:**

Maddy Elizabeth Sparks

☆ ☆

★ Ok ... I g2g! 'Cuz this is the end!

But wait ... Not the end 4ever!!!

Because you can get all the scoop on the web at www.limitedtoo.com

And get Tuned In to what's going on with The Too Crew!

♡Love,
    Maddy